ACE HITS
ROCK BOTTOM

Also by
Barbara Beasley Murphy and Judie Wolkoff

ACE HITS THE BIG TIME

ACE HITS
ROCK BOTTOM

Barbara Beasley Murphy • Judie Wolkoff

DELACORTE PRESS/NEW YORK

Published by
Delacorte Press
1 Dag Hammarskjold Plaza
New York, N.Y. 10017

Manufactured in the United States of America

First printing

Library of Congress Cataloging in Publication Data

Murphy, Barbara [date of birth].
Ace hits rock bottom.

Summary: Teenage movie actor Horace "Ace" Hobart and his New York gang, the Purple Falcons, get
involved in live theatre and an arson plot when they
take summer jobs at a home for retired actors.
[1. Gangs—Fiction. 2. Acting—Fiction. 3. Arson—
Fiction. 4. Old age—Fiction. 5. New York (N.Y.)—Fic-
tion] I. Wolkoff, Judie. II. Title.
PZ7.M948Ab 1985   [Fic]
ISBN 0-385-29412-3
Library of Congress Catalog Card Number: 85-3776

To Teddy, Mark, Bill, John, and Christopher
and especially to my brother Bill
—B.B.M.

With love to my two brothers, Jack and Walt.
—J.W.

Will you see the players well bestowed? Do you
hear, let them be well used;
for they are the abstract and brief
chronicles of the time.
—*Hamlet,* Act II, sc. 2, ll. 546–548

One

"Horace, get up!" Mom yelled from the back of The Pits.

"Gimme a break, it's early," I whined, pulling the pillow over my head. Didn't she know it was summer? Vacation? Sometimes I think she's forgotten who I am. ACE HOBART. "Hot Property." That's what Marilyn Maroon called me, and she was the director of the movie I was in.

When *Bound and Gagged* opened last February, it was a big hit and I was on my way to stardom. All kinds of people were after me. Teen magazine reporters. TV shows. Interviewers. I thought I was going to be a living legend like Matt Dillon, driving a red Trans Am. *Zzooom!* I'd fixed up my room to suit my new image and bought every imaginable gadget. And then a terrible thing happened. Overnight the movie disappeared. Two weeks after it opened.

"Y'know why? You had *poor distribution,* kids," Jerry Cone said, sadly shaking his big mop of curly hair at me and the other Falcons. They're my buddies—Freddy, George, J.D., and Slick—the gang of guys I was in the movie with. And Jerry Cone is our agent. "You make a film with a punk company like The Maroon Movie Machine and that's what you get," Cone told us. "No clout at the box office. Sign with me and I'll make you bigger stars than the ones in the Big Dipper. What you need in this business is a hot agent."

So we signed.

"Horace!" my mother yelled again.

And we go to auditions. But so far it hasn't done any good. Nobody wants gangs right now. Not even in commercials. Most people don't even recognize us.

"Horace!"

It was then that I realized Mom's gone back to calling me Horace instead of Ace.

"Horace, I mean it. Get up!" she yelled. "You're going out looking for a job today."

Her voice sounded closer so I yanked the sheet up to my neck. I couldn't risk letting her see my new pajamas in case she came in. "I can't go looking. I've got an audition."

The bedroom door banged open. "Horace, get out of that water bed right now or I'm going to drag you out!" she shouted. She marched inside, buttoning her Gristede's supermarket smock. She got a job there as a cashier last month to help pay off the installments on the Barcalounger and couch we got when the movie opened. When we thought we were going to be rich.

Her pale eyes were smoking. "Your dad and I have had it," she said. "Either you find a job today or I'm telling Mr. Papadopoulos you'll be working for him in the meat department. Starting tomorrow at seven-thirty A.M.!"

"Me? A butcher?" I winced, picturing my severed thumb getting wrapped up in a package of drumsticks. "Mom, how can I? I'm an actor."

"Actor?" she shrieked. "You've got the wrong word, Horace. You're a *debtor!* Look at the things you owe for . . . your water bed, those black sheets, that wall-mounted stereo over there, a tape deck, Atari set, no-fog clock, your chiming telephone, and heaven only knows how many Claude Clerc shirts."

"*Le* Clerc, Ma. Claude *Le* Clerc."

She took a deep breath and held it. "Horace," she said after a minute, "the charges on our Visa card are all yours. Twelve hundred and sixty-two dollars' worth! Your dad and I are completely unwilling and unable to cover those payments, and if you don't get a job to make that next one on July twelfth, the authorities are going to put you in jail next to your Uncle Jake. It's the same as stealing, Horace, not to pay your bills."

"I could pay them easy if you'd just give me the rest of my movie money."

"Not on your life. That money's for your education," she said. "It's staying in the money market fund. And furthermore, you're going to learn to be responsible. Don't you see what's happening to you, Horace? You get one fluke part in a movie and it ruins you. Now you're lazy and—"

My Danish phone on the nightstand chimed.

"Get it for me, would ya, Ma?"

She stared at me and didn't move. Neither did I. If I reached for it, I'd expose my pajamas. "Please, Ma? It might be Raven or the guys. Maybe my agent."

"*You* get it!"

"Nora!" I yelled for my little sister. "Come get my phone for me, would ya?"

Mom shook her head and sighed. "Never have I seen anyone so lazy."

"Nora!" I yelled again. Where was she?

"Your little sister left for *her* job two hours ago," Mom said, shoving her hands in her pockets. "She's not even eleven yet, but she understands the financial predicament the Hobarts are in. And *she's* saving *her* money. A dollar for each dog she walks, plus tips."

My phone chimed for about the eleventh time. "Ma, please? I'll miss my call."

"No!" she snapped. Then, without any warning, she reached down, ripped off my sheet, and started screaming. "Horace! Where'd you get *those?*"

"I . . . well . . . Bloomingdale's was having a sale. . . ."

"Bloomingdale's? With all the money we owe, you bought those? *Nylon zebra pajamas?* What did you do? Charge them?"

"Look, Ma . . . don't worry. They're not cheap or anything. They're silk. . . ."

"Silk?" She stepped back, squeezing her face into a painful knot. "Get those decadent Playboy p.j.'s off your young body!" she said as she started out of my room. "And be dressed in *five* minutes! You're coming to Gristede's with me this morning."

She was still watching me, to see what I'd do, so I got out of bed and dug through a heap of clothes I'd left on the floor and pulled out my *Oui!* jeans. Only a miracle could save me now, I thought. Then it happened. My phone chimed again.

This time I caught it on the second *boing.*

"Hey, kid," came a familiar voice on the other end. "Y'know who this is? Jerry. Jerry Cone as in ice cream, got it? And you're not exactly Tommy Tune, right? So where were ya when I tried calling a couple of minutes ago?"

"Oh, hi. In the, uh, bathroom . . . showering. Sorry. But nobody else, ha-ha, was here."

Mom was breathing down my neck. "That's a lie. You're learning to lie."

"You got something for me, Jerry? A job?" I said, desperately trying to get away from her.

"Hey, have I got something for you! Look, kid . . .
does a bear poop in the woods? Of course I got you a
job. An agent's always hustling. I got jobs for all you
Falcons. You're gonna take a little trip north today."

Two minutes, Mom was mouthing at me.

"Where? Uptown? You got a commercial for us?" I
asked, turning my back on her.

"A commercial? You think the big stuff falls out of
trees?" he shouted. "People break your door down
when you're Tim Hutton, not before, okay? What I got
is a little more basic. So grab a pencil and take down this
address."

I scribbled as fast as I could: *The Wartzburg . . .
number 1050 on the Grand Concourse. Director, Hannah Otterbridge.* When I hung up, I felt so happy, I
could've kissed Mom. "This time it's not an audition," I
told her. "It's a . . ."

With a look of frustration she'd turned and stomped
out of my room. "How can you still believe in that man,
Horace? How?"

"Ma, you don't understand," I called after her. "Acting's in my blood. I'd do anything to act. Give up my
life, my limbs, my blood, my—"

"Good-bye, Horace. I'm late for work and I'm leaving. Don't you dare come home till you have a job."

As soon as I heard the front door close, I dressed, ate a
quick La Yogurt breakfast, and decided to skip my
morning workout. What I needed—now that I was going back into show biz—was a Gravity Guide System.
There was a little slack in my abdominals, and my ham-
strings could use some stretching. Should I call Zero
down at the Eighth Street Jock Shop? Remind him I'd
left a deposit on one and to hurry up and send it?

I looked at my watch. Ten o'clock. I'd do it some

other time. I had to round up the Falcons for our one-thirty appointment.

"Ace, you lucky devil," I hooted as I looked in a mirror and ran a comb through my hair. "You're gonna be a star again."

TWO

Soon as I hit the street, I slapped on my black eyepatch. Not that I've had a horrid sty to cover lately. My patch just made a big hit when I was in my movie, is all.

I checked my watch again. If I moved fast, I figured I'd have time to stop by and see my girl, Raven, to let her in on the good news.

The door to her apartment building, two blocks from my house, was open when I got there. The new super, who was washing the glass in the door, recognized me and told me to go up. "Señorita Galvez is in," he said as I squeezed past him.

Raven's family's third-floor apartment with its lime-green walls and shaded windows was dark and cool. Her little sister, Sylvia, let me in and directed me to a couch covered with a flowered bedspread. I sat down easy so as not to mess it up.

"She'll be out in a minute," Sylvia said. "You mind sitting alone? I'm in the bathroom practicing my Suzuki violin." She turned and ran off to the little room next to the kitchen and slammed the door.

"Hey, play a little softer, would you please?" Violin squeaks get on my nerves, especially when I'm under pressure. Sylvia was nice, not at all like my sister, and she cut the decibels a good bit.

After a couple more minutes passed, I figured I ought to call Raven. "Hey, I haven't got much time," I hollered.

"Be there in a sec, Ace," she sang out down the hall.

"Raven, I don't mean to rush you but I've got a heavy day ahead. Important stuff. Hurry up, come on out."

I heard her firm high-heeled steps come tapping down the linoleum-covered floor of the hall. I swallowed and felt the usual rush of hot blood course through my veins. (That's a quote from the Nevada Culhane book I'm reading. It's hot off the press. I buy hardback now.)

Raven came in smiling, wearing a fire engine–red dress guarded at the neck by a silk scarf tied in a tight bow. I didn't know why she was all dressed up. I met her in the middle of the living room and reached out to touch her shoulder so I could lay claim to just a bit of her. But she backed off. Her beautiful dark eyes were sparking with fury.

"What's the matt—"

"What are you doing here in that patch? You said you had a heavy day . . . important stuff! You're supposed to be getting a job."

"Wait a minute . . . who are you, my mother?" I yelled back. She'd just squelched my romantic mood. "I don't have to answer to you."

She glared at me and nodded her head.

"No, I don't," I said.

She crossed in front of me and went to stand at the window, looking down at the street. "Ace, you said you were going to get a job this summer. You know, go back to being normal. Just look at how you've changed! When I first met you, you were natural and considerate. . . . Now you're spoiled."

"I'm not any different," I said, going to stand behind her. She backed away from the window and bumped into me where I'd strategically placed myself with open arms. "Oh! Get away!" she said.

"I came to tell you I got a job," I said, and explained that Jerry Cone was sending all of us Falcons to the Bronx to work in the Wartzburg Theater.

"In the Bronx!" she said. "I can't believe you're still listening to Jerry Cone, that cheapshot con artist! You guys are so gullible! He can tell you anything. You think you're going to get into another movie without even being trained as actors? Oh, quit fooling yourself, Ace. Please! It was a fluke—Marilyn Maroon, *Bound and Gagged!*"

"You've been talking to my mother!" I said. "We're going to work in a theater and *get* experience. Gimme a break, Raven!"

She sighed, took a jacket that matched her dress from the hall closet, and opened the front door. "The rest of your life isn't going to drop out of heaven, Ace," she said, going out ahead of me.

"Wait up, Raven, you don't understand . . ."

"Why don't you just grow up?" she shouted over her shoulder as she reached the street. An uptown bus had stopped at the corner. She hopped on without a word and was gone. Didn't even bother to tell me where she was going.

I knew where I was going. Up to the Dumont Health Club in Times Square, where the Falcons were working out. When *Bound and Gagged* premiered, the Dumont sent all five of us complimentary three-month memberships. When it was time to renew, everybody joined but me. I couldn't afford it. Neither could Freddy, J.D., George, or Slick, actually, but they did anyway.

The Dumont's a great place to meet people in show biz and pick up the news. I missed being part of it. When I got there, the main gym was jammed. Every

unemployed actor in New York spends his days in there, I think. And even some of the lucky working ones, like the Falcons would be when I found them.

Of all of us, Freddy Cruz is the farthest along in the Nautilus program. When I walked in, he was doing bench presses and J.D. was spotting for him. He's pressing over three hundred pounds already and his body shows it.

J.D. saw me right away. He was wearing his cutoffs and a red striped tank top. Sweat glistened on his smooth blue-black skin. He doesn't have that wild Afro haircut anymore with the zigzag part. Now he's close-cropped, conservative. Slick, on the other hand, went overboard and got a body perm.

"What's happening, Ace?" J.D. asked.

"Great news . . . can we call a meeting?" I said, looking around for the other Falcons. I could have sworn I saw Dustin Hoffman in the corner, working on his biceps. They weren't any more developed than mine, which I quickly pointed out to J.D. But he said it wasn't Dustin. Just one of his look-alikes.

"What kind of news, Ace?" Freddy grunted. He was holding the bar, exhaling, jabbing it high in the air, holding it there. The muscles in his throat bulged; a vein in his temple throbbed in his purple-red face.

"Jerry Cone called," I said. "Hey, Freddy . . . quick! Breathe in."

Slowly he brought the bar down, sucking in air like an asthmatic. I moaned and panted, watching him. He was always saying there was nothing to it. For him, maybe. I felt weak when he finished. "What's Cone got for us?" he said.

"Surefire jobs."

"Man, I'll believe that when I see it," said J.D.

"What is it, an audition at the Met?" said Freddy, sitting up. "Lemme hear you sing, J.D."

I went into the dance room next door to look for Slick and George. I only saw Slick. He was doing leg stretches on the barre, admiring himself in the mirrored wall like he was seeing Rudolf Nureyev. Slick wasn't working the Nautilus program anymore. He'd quit when a gorgeous ballet instructor told him he had the perfect body for entrechats and tour jetés. He can't even say the words right, but he's doing flying leaps all over the place and wearing a beige leotard and a one-strap top. It matches his beige face and hair so well, he looks naked.

"Hey, Slick, emergency meeting," I hollered in to him. "Come into the main gym."

He cleared his throat, but since he became a ballerina, or whatever you call him, he doesn't spit as much anymore. "Get George first, would ya, Ace? I wanna do a few pliés. Whaddya think?" he said, sliding his feet into second position.

That bugged me, but I went after George and found him where I thought I'd find him . . . doing aerobics with a bunch of Broadway chorus girls. He was wearing one of his Joe Weider weight-lifting suits. He'd bought one for every day of the week. Today's was pearl gray with wine and dark blue racing stripes flying across the back.

When George saw me, he winked. That meant I was supposed to notice that he was standing next to the stacked redhead he'd been mooning over the past two weeks.

"Her name's June Light," he whispered when I got him out in the hall. "She's an actress in soaps . . . I was just getting ready to ask her for a date."

I was ready to ask him how he was planning to pay for

it. Then I noticed his watch was gone. Obviously he'd pawned it. "Ask her out some other time," I said. "I'm calling an emergency meeting."

George's cold gray eyes narrowed. "Why? What's happening? You seen any Piranhas in our neighborhood, Ace?"

"Jerry Cone called. He's got us all jobs."

For a minute I thought George was going to cream me. He doesn't trust Cone. Can't even stand to hear his name mentioned. "Yeah? What's he got for us now?" he spit out. "Auditions for a Midas muffler commercial? We get to play the exhaust fumes or something?"

"Nope. No auditions, George. I swear. Cone's got us parts in a play. All we have to do is go see the director."

I doubt if I ever would've talked him into leaving June Light and his aerobics class if his Joe Weider suits had been paid for. But George was in hock worse than any of us. Really tough shape. Besides getting a water bed and stereo stuff, he'd gone ape and bought the deluxe Apple home computer. He thought he could program the best odds for horse races and win OTB every week. Smart as he is, it hadn't worked.

Important as getting jobs was, the Falcons wouldn't leave the Dumont till they showered and shampooed. We've become the cleanest, best-smelling gang in the city. Being movie stars got us into the habit. None of us even wear our black leather jackets much. We're into status labels and high fashion. J.D. shot a hundred bucks on two pairs of designer shades, French imports. Then they got stolen out of his gym locker. That's why he and the others carry their workout stuff back and forth in Adidas tote bags now.

I got a little impatient waiting for them to finish

grooming and come out to the lobby in their street clothes. "No more delays," I said. "The director's expecting us. We got to be in the Bronx by one-thirty."

"*The Bronx?*" they yelled.

"The currency there's the same," I said. "It pays for stereos and water beds just like Manhattan money. And the big Broadway stuff doesn't fall out of trees, know what I mean?" I was beginning to sound like Jerry Cone *and* my mother.

Nobody said anything except Slick. He whined that he was too hungry to take a subway ride without first getting "a little something" at the health food snack bar. We all said no.

"Not even a quick glass of Tiger's Milk?"

George dug into his Adidas bag and handed him a soybean and kelp cracker. "Eat it and shut up," he snapped. Slick munched quietly as we all headed for the Sixth Avenue subway.

"By the way, you talked to Raven lately?" Freddy asked me when we were buying our tokens.

"Yeah. A couple of hours ago."

"She tell you she got a job?"

Job! My heart sank. She must've landed the one she wanted at Los Caballeros restaurant. The thought of other guys drinking sangria, watching her stomping her feet doing a fiery flamenco dance, ripped me apart. "When is she starting?" I asked.

Freddy hopped into an uptown train and we all got on after him. "Today," he said. "She's reading novels to a rich man."

"Hey! What's the matter with him? Can't he read them to himself?"

"Not everything's in braille, Ace," George said. "The guy's blind."

Three

The subway we took to the Bronx didn't have working air conditioners. While it was moving, Freddy shoved open the end door to lead us into the next car. The tunnel air smelled corroded and I couldn't get the metal taste out of my mouth. The next car wasn't any cooler either.

Suddenly the train lurched and jerked to a stop, and the lights went out. "What's wrong?" I yelled. I didn't want to be stuck on a dark train, feeling like a poached egg in my jeans.

"The Piranhas are mugging underground," J.D. cracked with a nervous laugh.

It was five minutes until the lights came on and the train moved. Five minutes that gave us all a chance to think about the gang of tall mean guys from the Bronx we'd fought last year.

"This is it. Our stop," Freddy said as we pulled into 170th Street a half hour later. When we came up to street level, he swiveled his head 360 degrees to check it out.

It was my first time in the Bronx. I followed everyone down the street, hoping we'd see a famous landmark like Yankee Stadium. But the first thing that caught my eye was a poor shopping-bag lady picking through a trash can.

We were on the Grand Concourse, the main drag. It was busy with traffic and wide as a river. On each side were luxury buildings going to seed. A couple were

nothing more than burned-out shells. Fifty years ago, George told us, this was rich-man's-land. "Now most of the side streets are controlled by slumlords," he said.

Near a deli we ran into a crowd. "Look at that, Ace," J.D. whispered to me.

A guy had stacked three cardboard boxes to make a table. On the top he'd laid out three playing cards that he was switching fast while he talked even faster to the crowd. "Watch!" he called. "Ya play twenty, ya win forty. Watch!"

He flipped over the cards and I saw two black ones and the red ace of diamonds. "Pick the red one and you win," he shouted, turning them over and switching them around again. I was sure I knew which was the red ace. It had a little curl on the edge.

A girl in a yellow striped dress put down a twenty-dollar bill. Her face was quiet and thoughtful as she examined the backs of the cards. Then she pointed a long fingernail at the one I thought was the ace of diamonds and flipped it over.

"All *right!*" I said when she won.

The other Falcons gave me an edgy look. "Ya can't win at three-card monte," said Slick.

What did he know? I dipped my hand into my pocket, and just as I was ready to put down my money, I felt my arms getting yanked out of their sockets. George and Freddy both had me, dragging me down the street.

"Hey! What're you doing? Lemme go!"

"It's a *scam,* man," said George.

"Yeah? Well, maybe *you* don't know it, but I was a *whiz* at card tricks when I lived in Guttenberg, New Jersey!"

Slick seemed impressed. "You could win three-card monte, Ace?"

"Of course. Why not?" I twisted my head to look back, but the cardshark and crowd were gone. Two policemen stood where they'd been a minute ago.

I gave up struggling and started looking at the numbers on the apartment buildings. "What's the theater called, Ace?" said George.

"The Wartzburg. Number Ten-fifty."

"And what's the name of the play?" asked J.D.

"Jerry didn't say. But the director's name is Hannah Otterbridge. Ever heard of her?"

Freddy thought a minute. "Sounds familiar."

"Yeah," added Slick. "Maybe she's the one who did *Chorus Line.*"

Number 1050 was three blocks from the subway. The two buildings just before it were apartment buildings with torn, faded canopies. Both had seen far, far better days.

We cut around some little kids playing stickball on the sidewalk and there it was, the theater we'd been looking for. The Wartzburg. It was a huge white rambling Victorian mansion set way back from the street on its own parklike lawn.

"Must've been the home of a billionaire once," said George.

I nodded. The Wartzburg was the size of a small seaside hotel, old Atlantic City style. The lawn still looked good . . . flower beds, park benches, and bushes that were pruned to look like giant beach balls. Surrounding it all was a high spiked wrought-iron fence with a locked gate. I pressed the buzzer on the gate and a watchman, who'd eyed us from the window of a guard-

house inside, came out, jangling keys. He looked like a New York cop.

"What can I do for you?" he said, swelling his pecs.

The Falcons looked at me. I cleared my throat, and the foghorn voice I get when I'm nervous answered. "Mr. Jerry Cone sent us about jobs. We have an appointment with the director."

The guard gave us directions. We crossed the lawn and went up a flight of wooden steps onto the front porch. There was a row of green rockers with high backs, probably for the audience at intermission. Except for an old man sitting in one and rocking, they were empty. As I went by, I heard him say to himself in an odd voice, "Whar ma bleedin' from?" I looked at him; he gave me a great smile, and there wasn't a sign of blood. An actor practicing lines! I smiled back. We were going to be in the same theatrical company.

Inside the front door we found Miss Otterbridge's office. The Wartzburg smelled funny to me, like food and disinfectant. I thought they probably had a restaurant like the dinner theaters in the suburbs.

Miss Otterbridge, a beak-faced woman in the office, didn't hear us come in. A noisy fan whirred on her desk. Every time it turned to blow directly on her face, her short-cropped hair rose off her temples like sparrow's wings.

She *ain't no Marilyn Maroon,* Freddy mouthed. Our director on *Bound and Gagged* was really built.

When Miss Otterbridge finally looked up and saw us, she jumped. "Who let you in here?" she said, dropping her pencil on the floor.

Slick stooped to pick it up.

"The watchman did," Freddy said. "We're the actors Mr. Cone sent."

She took the pencil without thanking Slick and used the eraser end to push her glasses up her nose. For a minute she studied each of us. "I suppose you'll have to do," she said. Then she pointed the lead end of the pencil at Freddy and Slick. "You and you. You'll be the gardeners. Afternoon hours, so you can clear the tables after tea and set up for dinner."

Freddy drew in his chin. Slick squinted. Like me, I guess they felt confused. She was almost talking a different language.

"And you and you and you," she continued, jabbing the pencil toward J.D., George, and me, "you'll be the evening busboys. The job's seven days a week, six hours a day, minimum wages. Gardeners report for work at noon. Waiters at three. We supply white shirts and ties . . ."

"*Work?*" said Freddy.

"Report for *work?*" George repeated, cutting his eyes at me.

Without acknowledging any interruption, Miss Otterbridge continued, ". . . and you're expected to arrive neat and tidy with your hair combed. The Wartzburg maintains rigid standards. Any questions?"

"I've got one, Mrs. Otterbridge. Do the gardeners have many lines?" Slick asked.

"What do you mean by lines? And it's not *Mrs.!*"

"Sorry. Ms. Otterbridge, you kn—"

"No. Miss. Miss."

Slick started to stutter. "L-lines for the play we're supposed to be in. Do we have any, or are we just walk-ons?"

"*Parts? For a play?*"

The Falcons turned and glared at me.

I started smoothing my hair with my nervous hand.

"See . . . uh, you see, Mr. Cone . . . uh . . . led us to believe that we—"

"The Wartzburg is an actors' retirement home," Miss Otterbridge broke in. "If you are actors, you certainly should have heard of it. It's funded with money left by the late Chester Wartzburg, a patron of the arts during the Depression. He was in railroads. Thirty-eight of the most gifted and talented members of the American theater live here."

"But—"

"And furthermore, we hire *un*employed actors and actresses as waiters, gardeners, housemaids, et cetera, releasing them whenever they must go for auditions or take a role in a play. In that way we contribute to the American theater."

"Yeah?" said Slick, who was the only one who didn't look upset. Miss Otterbridge nodded. For a long minute nobody else spoke.

Finally J.D. said, "You mean you got openings for two gardeners to take care of the lawn and three busboys to set up and clear tables and—"

"And wash dishes and peel potatoes, et cetera," Miss Otterbridge added.

"Hey! Now, hold it," said George. "Thirty-eight people messing up a bunch of plates and cups and saucers is an awful lot of work for three guys, don't you think? Why can't gardeners do some of them dishes?"

"Gardeners *do* do dishes. They do the *tea* dishes," Miss Otterbridge said, sounding surprised, as though it was a silly question.

Slick groaned. Freddy told Miss Otterbridge we needed five minutes for a short conference outside the office to discuss her offer. "Don't take long!" she

warned. "Hundreds of unemployed actors would be glad to work here."

I felt a dagger-like elbow in my side from George, took the hint, and followed the guys out to the porch. They turned on me suddenly, and their angry faces blocked out the sky and lawn behind them. "Now, wait a minute . . ." I said, backing up a step.

George swatted my shoulder. *"You! You* wait a minute! You brought us all the way up here for a job like *this!"*

"How could you be so dumb, Ace?" J.D. said. "I thought we taught you all we knew."

"Why didn't you *ask* what kind of job it was that Cone was shipping us up here for?" Freddy growled.

"Any jackass would know there aren't theaters in the Bronx!" George said.

"I can't work as a busboy or a gardener. I don't know a rosebush from spaghetti sauce!" J.D. said.

"You're not going to take the jobs?"

"Shoot, Ace, this could ruin our image," Slick said.

All of a sudden Freddy turned on George. "Hey! Why didn't *you* say it, if you knew there wasn't no theaters in the Bronx?"

"Freddy!" I jumped in. "Who would have thought an *agent* would be calling to send his actor clients to work shoveling hash to old folks? Cone fooled us all!"

"I would've!" George bellowed. "I told you you can't trust agents. Just last month in *Newsweek* I read that. Geez, don't you guys read anything?"

"What'd Cone say, actually?" Freddy said to me.

I tried to remember. "He gave me the director's name, the address, and name of the . . . uh, this place." The Falcons stared at me. "Well, we got to make a decision," I said. I was willing to forget the whole

thing, give up the job, and let the Visa people foreclose
on my water bed and other stuff. And then I remembered Mom's parting words and knew I had no choice.

"Man, we got to take these jobs!" Freddy said suddenly, biting the words like they were a piece of tough
meat. "We gotta do it. No *dinero,* no life! I'm half a guy
without money."

"Maybe we can still find something else. . . ." Slick
offered.

"Shut up!" J.D. said, looking like he wanted to cry.
"My folks are going to throw me out if I don't make
some money. They don't like the way I'm using my
time, either. *'Working out!'* my mom said this morning,
like it was some big sin."

Freddy took a deep breath. "This is it," he said, opening the screen door.

Slick, J.D., and I walked through, but George stayed
where he was. "It'll kill me to take this kind of work. I'm
leavin'."

"Who you kiddin'?" J.D. said, laughing. "You got the
most bills!"

"I got my pride, too. I can't baby-sit for a bunch of
toothless old . . ." George made a mean gesture and
leaped off the porch.

"George!" I hollered, watching him run across the
lawn. But he was gone. The rest of us looked at each
other.

"Sorry. I can't wait any longer," Miss Otterbridge
said, coming out onto the porch. "What's your decision?"

Slick cleared his throat. "You're on, ma'am."

Miss Otterbridge's face relaxed into a nice smile.
"We'll need a fifth person," she said, realizing there

were only four of us left. "Try to bring someone else with you tomorrow."

"Yeah, sure," said Freddy.

"Good. Now, if you'll all come with me, I'll give you a tour of the Wartzburg." She started down the porch steps, then turned. "But first I have a personal question. Mr. Cone mentioned that you young men appeared in a movie last year. Would you tell me which one? The residents would be interested."

Freddy's face lit up. *"Bound and Gagged.* Did you see it?"

"No, I missed it."

"Too bad, 'cause it was real good," Slick said. "You would've enjoyed watchin' the Ace here when he got his throat slashed."

Four

The first thing we saw was the yard. The Wartzburg's grounds, Miss Otterbridge explained as she unlocked a toolshed in the back, consisted of one-point-three acres of lawn and "precious" plantings that needed constant, rigorous attention.

"Those machines you see hanging on hooks are the double-edged hedge trimmers," she said, pointing at the wall. "They have two-point-two-amp motors, giving you three thousand cutting strokes a minute. Gifts from the Actors Guild. Now, then, I assume you young men know how to operate the self-propelled lawn mowers?"

She meant Freddy and Slick, the gardeners. Both of them gave me evil looks. "Oh, yeah, sure! Nuttin' to 'em," Freddy said.

Going up the back steps to the kitchen, I stayed away from him.

"Smells like hot Crisco . . . or donuts!" Slick whispered. I was hungry.

"Mister Raymond!" Miss Otterbridge called, opening the door. Her voice echoed in the huge steel and white-tile kitchen. A short peach-skinned man who looked about forty, wearing an apron and a tall white hat, stopped his food processor and turned. He'd been pureeing cooked vegetables.

"This is our chef, Raymond Emanuel. Mister Raymond, these are our new busboys and gardeners." He raised a mournful face to us, and Miss Otterbridge was quick to add, "A chef's most precious possessions are his

mixing arm and his ability to stand long hours before a stove."

I felt J.D. nudge me. The chef's feet were encased in elephant-size Space Shoes built to conform to his bulging bunions.

Mister Raymond turned back to his vegetables, and Miss O. gave us her kitchen crash-course on how to compact a trash bag of garbage, where to locate and store dinnerware, and how to operate an institutional dishwasher. The washer, I was relieved to see, did a set of fifty dishes in a swoop. But, of course, no pots and pans. That was a job for the busboys. We were each given our own scouring pad and dish.

"Gee, thanks a lot, Miss Otterbridge," Slick said.

Now we were ready for the course on table setting in the dining room. "J.D., you carry up the plates; Freddy, you and Slick carry silver." She gave them loaded trays and told me to hold out my arms for the linens. "These are pure damask."

And, I wanted to add, *weigh a ton!* I staggered up the stairs behind her, trying not to trip and holding the tablecloths high so they wouldn't sweep the floor.

Miss Otterbridge led us through the swinging doors into the dining room. Our jaws dropped open at the sight. Wine-red carpeting, dark wood paneling, velvet drapes, and crystal chandeliers, one for each of the six round tables in the room.

"By the way, I ain't seen any of the old folks who are supposed to live here," J.D. said.

"Most of our residents—*not* old folks, J.D.—are just finishing their siestas. Please watch your diction, grammar, and vocabulary."

A red light flashed over an intercom panel by the buffet. Miss Otterbridge pressed a button. "Otter-

bridge speaking." She pointed me to a mahogany table near the window, where I began to unfold a tablecloth.

"Miss Otterbridge!" came a voice that didn't sound old to me. "Miss Orient is threatening to have the vapors if I don't give her her whiskey. What'll I do?"

"You know the rules. Give her a cup of tea."

"Should I come down and get it?"

"No, Leslie, I'm going to put wings on a cup and fly it up to you," snapped Miss Otterbridge.

That just killed Slick, who was helping with the cloths. A few seconds later a dark-haired young woman wearing a candy-striped dress that matched Mister Raymond's apron came running through the dining room on the way to the kitchen.

"Hey! Weren't you auditioning for the Dinky Danish commercial last month?" J.D. called after her.

"Yeah, you too?"

"Yeah, we didn't get it."

"Me either," she said, disappearing into the kitchen.

"Now then, back to business," said Miss Otterbridge. "Which of you young men can tell me where the bread plates go?" None of us answered. "On the left! *Always* on the left."

Everybody had had a turn setting a complete place setting, right down to the dessert fork, when I heard a floorboard creak behind me. I turned in time to see a wheelchair zip out of sight behind a plant in the corner.

"Don't tell them where I am," whispered a distinguished-looking white-haired man, peering at me from behind the leaves of a ficus tree.

"Tell who?" I said.

"Twiddle-dee-dum and Twiddle-dee-dee," he said with a crisp British accent.

I thought he was cuckoo until I saw two twiggy old ladies pitter-pattering around in the hall outside the dining room. Neither of them was much bigger than Nora. The one in the flowered housecoat opened a coat closet; poked and jabbed around the bottom with a wire coat hanger. "He's not in there," she said, slamming the door.

"I knew that!" said the one with the dyed orange hair.

She had already spotted us and had backed up behind the archway to the dining room, spying around the corner on us with one eye. It gave me the creeps, but I pretended not to notice.

I folded a napkin and set it on my table. Crap! Now the old lady in the flowered housecoat had spotted us. She was backing up to spy on us from the other side of the archway! I knew just how the poor old guy in the wheelchair felt.

"I think we should go in and introduce ourselves, Flora," said the lady with the orange hair. "The one with the big muscles could play Stanley Kowalski for us."

"Not now, Gayle. I can't meet men in my lounging clothes."

They whispered back and forth, arguing, and I just kept right on setting my table. So far, nobody else had seen them. Freddy was asking me which side Miss Otterbridge had said the bread-and-butter plates should go on, and Miss Otterbridge was making Slick redo his silverware. Apparently he'd put the spoons next to the forks.

At the table next to mine, J.D. was humming "Did You Have to Break My Heart in Splinters?" He'd been

humming it for two weeks straight and it was driving
me crazy.

I glanced over at the doorway to see how the argu-
ment was coming along, but the two old twiggy ladies
had disappeared.

"All right, Cecil. They're gone. You can come from
behind that plant now," Miss Otterbridge said.

J.D. stopped humming, and we all watched as the
wheelchair zipped out of hiding and down the middle
of the dining room. The old guy maneuvered it like he
was a race-car driver, then circled around my table,
stopping just an inch away from my foot. I thought he
was going to thank me for not stooling on him.

"But that I am forbid to tell the secrets of my prison
house, I could a tale unfold whose lightest word would
harrow up thy soul, freeze thy young blood, make thy
two eyes, like stars, start from their spheres . . ." he
said in a voice so tortured, I felt my skin crawl.

I waited for him to go on, but he spun his chair
around and shot it out of the dining room.

Miss Otterbridge looked enraptured by the whole
scene. "The gentleman you just saw," she said in a rev-
erent tone, "is the greatest Shakespearean actor of his
day . . . perhaps the greatest of all time. *Sir Cecil Bancroft!* Knighted in 1939 by the king of England."

"King? I thought England had a queen," said Slick.
"The one named after a ship."

Miss Otterbridge's smile was gone. "The queen was
not a queen in 1939! She was a princess. Her father was
the king."

"Ohh. Now I get it," said Slick.

"What I want to know," Freddy said, "is what he
meant by 'prison house.' You keep him locked up
here?"

"Who? The king?" said Slick.

"No! That guy Sir Cecil!" barked Freddy. *"Estúpido!* Didn't you hear what he was saying to Ace? That the secrets of his prison house would freeze our blood. What did he *mean* by that, Miss Otterbridge?"

"He was quoting *Hamlet!"* she barked, even louder than she'd barked at Slick. "Now, finish your tables and I'll introduce you to the people you'll be serving."

"What about that cute dish who came down for a cup of tea? Can we meet her, too?" J.D. asked.

Miss Otterbridge brushed a wisp of hair off her face. "If you finish your work quickly."

We did, and she took us to the second-floor sun-room where the Wartzburg residents congregate between naps and teatime. On the way upstairs, we heard somebody plunking out an old-time rinky-dink song on a tinny piano. A gutsy female voice was belting out the words, but I couldn't make them out till we hit the landing.

> . . . *my hot tamale went chili on me,*
> *So baby if you know a pepper that ain't pickled,*
> *It'd make me oh so tickled if you . . .*

The last line was so dirty I was embarrassed to look at Miss Otterbridge. She didn't strike me as the type who'd approve.

"Hey! Look who's playing. That's PeeWee Hooker!" J.D. said when we all went in. A little black guy sitting at the piano, wearing a faded old derby, glanced up. "I recognized his music right off. My old man's got a bunch of your records, sir," he hollered to the little guy. "Hey!"

PeeWee tipped his hat, then hunched over the keyboard and began playing the "Jelly Roll Blues." J.D.

couldn't stop grinning. The rest of us couldn't stop staring at what was lying lengthwise across the top of the piano: a barrel-bottomed lady with clusters of platinum ringlets, slabs of makeup, and a long yellow dress that hugged her body like a banana peel.

"Pearl! Off! Get *off* that piano!" Miss Otterbridge shouted.

The corners of Pearl's painted lips twisted into an evil smile, and she snapped open a black sequin fan. Pee-Wee took his cue, shifting his fingers into a new tune. "Ohhhhh the cowwww kicked Nelllll-y in the bellll-y in the barn," they belted out together.

The others in the room weren't as lively. By the window, rocking in a green wicker rocker, was the same man we'd seen rocking on the porch. Near him, on a couch, was a woman snoring with her mouth open. The rest—maybe nine or ten folks—sat so still, they looked stuffed.

Pearl Orient sat up and then kneeled on one knee on the piano as if she wanted to stand up now. I felt scared the whole thing was going to collapse with her.

"Don't you dare, Pearl! I mean it!" Miss Otterbridge was shouting. "You do, and I'll have you *evicted!* Immediately!"

Just then Leslie, the cute dark-haired girl we'd seen in the dining room, came into the sun-room, supporting a frail, tottering old woman, who was talking to herself.

"Miss Orient, please! Don't do that," Leslie said.

Pearl raised up and planted her feet on the piano, a triumphant smile on her face.

"I said I'd talk to Miss Otterbridge about spiking your tea."

"I'll do my own kind of talking," Pearl said, turning her giant backside to all of us.

"Please, Miss Orient . . . don't. I need this job."

Leslie had really won J.D. over. "I just can't figure how she didn't get the Dinky Danish commercial," he whispered to me.

"Get down," Miss Otterbridge screamed, "or I'll have Mister Raymond and Alfonso pull you down!"

Pearl ignored her. "Okay, little daddy," she called over her shoulder to PeeWee, "hit the big number."

PeeWee's thumbnail skidded down the keys and stopped at middle C, then he started hammering out one of those *pra-ba-boom* strip numbers. Pearl grunted each time her bottom swung with the rhythm, and one of the gloves she'd been wearing sailed through the air, landing on the floor in front of Miss Otterbridge's feet.

"Pearl! You take off *one more item of clothing* and I'm calling the board of directors. Now off! Get off that piano!" Miss Otterbridge wasn't shouting anymore, but her voice was sharper than a switchblade.

"On one condition," said Pearl. "You gotta give me back that bottle of whiskey you stole. I need it for medicinal purposes. I got a bad heart."

"We'll discuss the matter later. In my office."

The answer seemed to satisfy Pearl. She got off the piano by stepping onto the keys, then down onto Pee-Wee's bench. "Tonight?" she asked when her feet touched the floor.

"*Tomorrow!*" Miss Otterbridge said.

I had a feeling they had this tug-of-war going on between them all the time.

"Fortunately," Miss Otterbridge said as she led us away from the piano, "we won't be getting more of those Ziegfeld Follies girls. Most of them are dead." She looked at her watch. "And unfortunately, thanks to Pearl, I won't have time to show you young men the

prize of the Wartzburg—our legendary Barrymore Little Theater."

"You show movies?" asked Slick.

"We have an annual Dramafest. And on our stage you'll see the crème de la crème of the performing artists—our very own residents and staff."

I was relieved we didn't have time to see more of the Wartzburg. The place was getting to me. We left Miss Otterbridge at the landing and took to the stairs like we were evacuating a burning building. At the bottom, we hurried past Leslie and her frail companion.

"See you tomorrow," said J.D.

"Maybe," added Freddy.

The frail woman stared at Slick as if she was trying to place him. Then suddenly her eyes sparkled and she extended her hand. "This has been a very great honor, a very great honor indeed, Mr. President. How is Mrs. Coolidge?"

Slick took her hand, but looked helplessly at Leslie. "Huh? What does she mean?"

"Play along with her. Say Mrs. Coolidge is fine," Leslie whispered.

"Mrs. Coolidge is fine," Slick repeated.

The old woman curtsied. "Please tell her that Belva Bithell, the 'It' girl, sends her regards."

"Oh, sure . . . no sweat."

"Thank you very much, Mr. President."

"What's eatin' ya, Freddy?" Slick said.

No answer.

We were going out the Wartzburg's gates. At four in the afternoon the Grand Concourse was crowded with grouchy-looking denizens. I heard the sound of fire engine sirens and looked down the street. No sign of a fire, but way down in the next block I spotted a sign that said EAT. I hoped we were going to stop. I was starved.

"Sumpin' wrong?" Slick said again.

Freddy scowled, saying nothing.

A cold mood had come over my gang. They turned and headed on together, stopping when they came to the EAT sign, and went through the door without a word to me.

It was La Bombola China Grande. A poster in the window showed an Oriental man wearing a sombrero. Coming out of his mouth was a balloon with the words *Buena Comida*. It was Chinese-Cuban. I'd never eaten in a restaurant like this in my life. But hunger poked me like a stick. Even though I felt like leaving them and going home alone, I followed the Falcons in. They took the three empty stools at the counter. I stood. A grungy guy in a grungy apron recommended rice and beans.

"*Colorados*," he said. "Berry fine *colorados*."

So we all had pink beans and runny yellow sauce, deep-fried egg rolls on the side with duck sauce, chow mein noodles, and shredded iceberg on the top. The only vacant seat left was in a phone booth in the back,

so I took my plate there to eat. A buzzing fly dropped onto the beans but didn't stay. I ate where he'd been too.

Feeling lonely, I started to think about that dumb jerk Calvin Feckleworth in Guttenberg, New Jersey, my old hometown. Maybe I'd call him and set up something for the weekend, see old friends . . . then I remembered . . . I didn't have weekends anymore. . . .

The door of La Bombola China Grande slammed. "Falcons!" an eerily familiar voice rang out. "What're you dudes doing here?"

I recognized the strangulated tones of Stab the Piranha. I stuck my head out of the phone booth and saw him looming over Freddy, J.D., and Slick like the atom bomb cloud. He was a member of the tall gang us Falcons had outfoxed last September way down in lower Manhattan. He'd grown, I noticed, from eight feet to ten. Stab!

A monster as tall but twice as wide had followed him in, shaking the floorboards. He was the one called Cannibal. Behind him was Turtle with the miserable complexion and the dented nose. When the counterman saw them, he nodded in a friendly but nervous way.

"Where are your little pals? George and the big star, Ace?" Stab said to Freddy. They hadn't seen me.

I shrank into the phone booth and didn't move. Rats! I hadn't eaten the egg roll, saving it for last; now I couldn't.

Freddy didn't answer. "What're you guys doing here?" Stab said.

Finally Slick said, "Uh, just visiting."

The Piranhas looked doubtful. There was a hot and

sweaty silence; everybody took everybody else's mea-
sure. We were in Piranha territory, their turf.

Outside the restaurant were three other tall guys,
looking in. I swallowed and glanced down. A cockroach
came slithering out from under my boot and escaped
into the drek in the corner.

"Visiting who?" Cannibal said.

"Somebody's grandma," J.D. snapped.

"Whose?" Turtle said, reaching up to stretch his tur-
tleneck collar away from his leathery neck and fanning
himself there with his hand. It was smooth and pudgy
with no visible knuckles.

"Uh . . . Slick's grandma, she's at the Wartz—"
Freddy broke in mid-sentence. *"On* the Grand Concourse. She's ill, very, very sick, poor woman. Dying."

"Huh! Well, what happened to show biz? You guys
were into a big career?" Stab's eyes narrowed. He
picked up Freddy's fork and leafed through the rice on
his plate, found a chili pepper, and popped it into his
mouth.

"We're making another movie," Slick said. "Didn't
you hear?"

J.D. slid off his stool, planted his feet on the floor, and
stood as tall as he could. "Tomorrow we're off on location."

"That's right, yeah . . . *Bermuda,"* Slick said.

The Piranhas backed off a hair.

"With Brookie Shields," said J.D.

The Piranhas' mouths dropped open. So did mine.
Stab let out a whistle. "Son of a ¢%#*X!" he said.
"Straight?"

As if on signal the door opened. Two skyscraping
girls, ugly as sin, in high plastic platform sandals,
clomped in.

"Are you telling us straight?" Stab said again. The girls, punk rockers in satin pants gathered at the ankles, with spiked hair dyed orange and blue, gazed at Stab while he spoke and then at the Falcons.

Freddy opened his palms in front of them.

J.D. said, "Would we lie?" and Slick crossed his heart.

The girls laughed a laugh that started in their throats, ran up the walls and over the ceiling. I shrank into the corner of the phone booth and peeked out again.

There was a hollow silence.

Stab and Turtle looked at the girls, who were grinning.

"Flame and Ember," Cannibal said.

The punk rockers took boxes of kitchen matches out of their bags and one of them struck a match. She stared at J.D. while it burned down to her black lacquered nails. She slowly blew it out. I shivered. The girl beside her lit another match and while it was flaming, passed her bare wrist through it. She must be Flame, I thought.

Stab leaned toward the Falcons, who were huddled together like a frozen blob. "If we discover you are making this up, Falcons, we're going to nuke your . . ."

I swallowed and shriveled into my corner. A minute later I heard the door open and then close. Whew! They had all left!

I crashed out of the phone booth, shrieking, "Freddy! Let's get outta here before those big ugly creeps come ba—"

I stopped dead. The female devils were still in here! When they saw me, they let out another of their maniacal laughs, and one of them pointed her long, sharp fingernail at my eyepatch.

"What do we have here, a winky one-eye?" said the girl I thought was Flame.

I shot out the door of La Bombola China Grande, not caring if the Falcons thought I was a coward. But when I glanced back, they were right behind me. They looked as scared as I was. We didn't slow down until we were a stone's throw from the subway. We skidded around the corner to the steps of the station.

"I thought you guys were never going to get here!" George said, lurching back into the doorway he'd lurched out of when we flew past. Everybody, surprised out of their birds, stared at him.

"I was waitin' for you. What took you so long? You can't believe what they were trying to get me to sign up for in there." He motioned his thumb at the storefront sign behind him.

"What does BMYL stand for?" Slick said.

"Bronx Model Youth League, would you believe!" said George. "They were feeding me graham crackers and Kool-Aid and . . ."

"Come on!" said Freddy, grabbing his wrist. "Tell us about it on the subway."

We started down the stairs. George's mouth kept running. ". . . and a woman named Iris Welch wanted me to sign a pledge for my salvation!"

"Why didn't you just go home?" J.D. asked.

"I couldn't. I lost all my money; in fact, I need to borrow a subway token," he said when we got to the turnstile.

I gave him one. "How'd you lose your money?"

"A guy cheated me at three-card monte."

"You're too smart for that, man," Freddy said.

We waited on the platform for the train to take us back home to Manhattan. When it came, we got into

the car and the door closed, sealing us in, safe from whatever was outside.

Then we told George about our meeting with the Piranhas, and the ugly punk girls.

"Wheewwwwww! Well, that's it!" Slick announced. "If the Piranhas and those freaks know we're here, we *can't* take those jobs."

"Whaddya mean, we can't take the jobs?" George said. "We have to take 'em. They're all we can get." He slumped into a seat.

Someone had left a newspaper behind on the seat next to me. The headline read BRONX ARSON SUS-PECTED! I started to read the article, but J.D.'s words interrupted my train of thought.

"Those punk mamas are going to mess us up. George, you missed it! You should have seen those skyscrapers!"

"Nine feet tall, at *least*. We think they're the Piranhas' Ladies Auxiliary," Freddy said.

"Only they're not ladies," Slick put in.

Freddy leaned over and turned his head to look at us. The muscles in his arms rippled. He couldn't be scared of anybody. But deep down I knew, we all knew, the Piranhas were dangerous, scary. So what if we'd outwit-ted them in a burned-out school building in Manhattan last fall? We didn't stand a flea's chance in the Bronx's Fort Apache, or whatever they called their battle-ground up here.

"The only thing we gotta do," said Freddy, "is to get up to the Wartzburg every day without that gang see-ing us. It's only a matter of blocks between the subway and the old folks place. We've just gotta make plans."

Everybody looked at each other, faces as blank as the bottoms of soda cans.

"So what's yer idea, Freddy?" Slick asked.

"I'm thinkin'."

"Yeah?" George said.

"Well?" said J.D.

Freddy wrinkled his face hard, his eyes beady with thought. The train, hurtling along the tracks across the bridge over the East River separating the Piranhas' mean Bronx from our Manhattan, rocked back and forth. We all leaned together, waiting for Freddy to come up with something.

"Crap!" he said. "I can't think of anything."

555-9310. I didn't even have to look the number up. It was engraved on my brain—555-9310. The Rising Star Talent Agency.

I put my money in the slot, waited for the dial tone, then dialed. It was ringing. Boy, just you wait, Mr. Jerry *as-in-dairy* Cone *as-in-ice cream!* Who do you think you are, huh? Sending us, the Purple Falcons, up to an old folks home. We're actors. Movie star actors! And we demand . . .

"Hello. Rising Star Talent Agency. Miss Winkler speaking."

"Oh . . . ha-ha . . . hi there, Miss Winkler. Could you put Jerry on the line?"

"Who's calling, please?"

"Umm . . . Ace. Tell him Ace."

"Ace who?"

"Ohh, uhh, Hobart. Tell him Ace Hobart. Please."

"Are you one of our clients, Mr. Hilbert?"

"Hobart. Umm, yes. Yes, I am. Six months now."

"One moment, please."

Five-minute pause. I had to put more money in the slot. Was I gonna tell him a thing or two!

"So sorry to keep you waiting, Mr. Hobart, but Mr.

Cone just now stepped out for lunch. May I take a message?"

"Message? Umm . . . naw. No thanks. I'll call tomorrow."

I hung up, came out of the phone booth, and looked at my watch. *Lunch? At this hour?* It was almost five-thirty. Why was he eating lunch now?

Six

"Come on, Horace . . . dinner's ready," Mom called.

When I walked into the kitchen to sit down, she was setting a steaming casserole of leftovers on the table. "Ewwww, sick," Nora whined. "What's *that?*"

Dad picked up the serving spoon next to it. "Slumgullion . . . specialty of the house, that's what!"

We all watched as he plunged the spoon into the congealed mass of gummy noodles, born-again vegetables, and last Sunday's tuna-bake. Mom looked ready to cry. "If any of you think it's easy to plan meals on our food budget, you're wrong," she said.

Dad let the gummy mass on the spoon plop onto his plate. "You call *this* a meal, Flo?"

"I know I'm not eating it," said Nora. "I'm fixing myself a bowl of cornflakes."

"You'll eat what the rest of us are eating or you won't eat!" Mom roared.

Here we go again, I thought. Nora whining, Mom crying, and Dad crabbing again about his job as a telephone repairman.

"Twenty years I've been at it," he was saying, "busting my chops doing overtime and working weekends. And where has this rat race got me?" His eyes traveled from the blob on his plate to the dead ivy hanging over a sinkful of dirty dishes. "Maybe we should get out of this asphalt jungle, move . . . go out west to . . ."

"Move?" Mom cried. "Are you out of your mind, Barney? We moved last year! Because *you* wanted a

change, *we* had to leave our nice house in New Jersey, *come* to this awful city, take this wretched apart—"

". . . a place like Wyoming," he went on, like he hadn't heard her. "All that land's just . . ."

"*Wyoming?* Ewwww, sick! Wolves . . . buffalo! Poison water! I know I'm not moving," said Nora. "I'll stay here and get my own apartment!"

"All that land's just sitting out there, waiting for a smart developer to come along," he started again, ignoring both of them. "Who knows? With a couple of hot tips and a few good contacts, we might make ourselves a bundle. Jake knows an inmate who knows somebody who—"

Whamm! Mom slammed her hand on the table. In or out of prison, Dad's younger brother, Jake, always has a get-rich-quick scheme. Even when he was in the merchant marine, before he went into illegal gambling— even before he went into income tax evasion—he was scheming.

"Ha-ha . . . now, Flo, I know what you're thinking," Dad said. "Just because Jake and I lost a little money on those pop-up umbrella hats he brought back from Japan . . ."

Mom's whole body had gone rigid. "A *little* money, Barney? You bought *five hundred* of those hats! They were going to sell like hotcakes . . . make us a fortune! And where are they? Mildewing in your sister-in-law's basement in Hoboken!"

"Uh-uh. Not all of them," Nora said, reaching up into the cupboard for the box of cornflakes. "Aunt Betty gave Horace a couple. He was the only person stupid enough to like the dumb things."

Whamm! Now Dad's hand slammed on the table. "You keep out of this! And put that box away! Your

mother fixed a delicious dinner." He forced a forkful
into his mouth, then turned to Mom. "Flo, think of the
future! Think what wide-open spaces would do for the
Hobarts. If I borrowed on my life insurance, we could
get a few acres . . . raise some beef cattle."

"Over my dead body!" Mom yelled. "The Hobarts
are going to stay put, work, save, eat leftovers, and pay
bills. And Horace is going to help out by taking that job
at Gristede's!" Her pale eyes fixed on me as if I was the
last person she could count on. "Aren't you, Horace,
honey?"

Now Dad's eyes were fixed on me like I was a traitor.

"Well, I, uh . . ." I hadn't had a chance to tell them
about my job at the Wartzburg. I didn't know where to
begin. "I . . . uh . . ."

"Horace, you dope!" Nora screamed as she poured
milk on her cornflakes. "If you say no and we have to
move to dumb Wyoming, I'll never tell you who called
today! *Never!*"

"Who? Raven?"

"Try and get it out of me. Just try!"

"Ahh, so you kind of go for the idea of a little spread
out in Wyoming, eh, son?" Dad was smiling at me.

"Horace, you rat . . . you dirty rat!" said Nora.

I looked at Mom, not saying anything, just picking at
her gummy noodles. "Ma, look, I'm sorry. But I can't
take that job . . . I, uh . . ."

"You horrible, no good, lousy, flea-bitten, rotten,
nincompooping, dirty, *dumb* rat!"

". . . it's like this, Ma. My agent got me a job. A good
job. Great opportunity. Starting tomorrow I'll be working at a . . . well, a place for actors. It's up in the
Bronx."

"Okay, Horace. I take it back. You're not a rat."

"The Bronx?" said Mom. "Why, Horace? Why would you want to go all the way up there? Gristede's is right here in our neighborhood."

"Mom! I'm an *actor!*"

With that, Dad got up, dumped his blob of casserole in the garbage, then poured himself a bowl of corn-flakes while Nora sat down to eat hers. If Mom hadn't been staring at me, I would have poured myself one too.

"Your agent got you an *acting* job?" she said.

"Well, not exactly . . . but it's for actors in between acting jobs. Helping other actors. Old actors. Famous actors. It's an actors' old folks home, actually. Who called me, Nora?" I said quickly, to change the subject. "Raven? Am I supposed to call her back?"

"If you make me tell you now, you'll be sorry," she said.

"Tell me!"

"Okay . . . it's your funeral! It was a guy named Zero, and he said the thingamajig with boots you ordered to hang upside down with came in. They're coming COD and . . ."

Crap! My Gravity Guide System.

". . . can you bee-lieve it, Mom? Horace is paying a hundred and eighty-six dollars for them!"

"Horace! With our bills?" Mom shrieked. "Barney, do something! Say something!"

"*Hor—*"

"Look, don't worry, Dad. I'll call and cancel. I'll call tomorrow. I'll . . ."

Whew! What luck. The phone was ringing. I didn't care if I had a collect call from a mass murderer.

Fortunately, it was only Freddy. He said he had a lot of things on his mind and wanted to get together to talk.

"Ace, think you could meet me at the north gate of Gramercy Park in an hour?" he asked.

"Now's better," I said, listening to the furor going on in the kitchen over my COD order.

I decided not to go back out there. "An emergency's come up . . . I'll be home in a couple of hours," I hollered as I ran out the door. It was slammed shut behind me before Dad could say, *You get back in here!* and I flew down the stairs.

What was on Freddy's mind? I wondered when I hit the corner of 23rd and Third. I'd never known him to get together alone with anybody to rap before. He's the private type; Mr. Muy Macho, Raven calls him. To let off steam, he usually does something physical like mashing cans. If he's really ticked off, he'll maul something big like a bus bumper.

I felt special that he'd singled me out to talk to.

When I got to the park, it was still light. I could see him near the gate, leaning at an angle against the spiked iron fence. Only his shoulders were touching the fence, and he looked like a flying buttress. I waved, then he waved. He didn't appear to be agitated. He wasn't crunching rocks under his boot heels or anything.

"You wanna walk or sit?" he said when I got up to him.

"Sit."

"The gate's locked. Let's climb the fence and sit on a bench."

I shrugged to let him think I thought scaling five feet was no sweat. Actually, it wasn't for him. He just chinned himself to the top rail, vaulted over, and came down on the other side as smooth and easy as a cat

walking over a pencil. I tried copying him and nearly impaled myself.

"Your problem is your shoulder joints ain't loose, Ace," he said while I was still perched up there on two spikes. "You need brachiation . . . body suspension from the arms. Do it twenty minutes a day and it'll build you up."

"Yeah, sure," I panted.

To get down, I had to step into the stirrup he made by cupping his hands together, then he lowered me to the ground.

"I mean it," he said. "You gotta hang every day for twenty minutes."

Instead of sitting on a bench, we ended up sprawled out on the grass near the little kids' sandbox, watching the sun set behind the Manhattan skyline.

"Wouldn't look the same anywhere else, huh, Ace?" he said as we shared a bag of banana chips he'd brought with him. "Kinda like a big old Florida navel orange going down behind a bunch of little purple boxes."

I felt a real pang zip through me when he said that. New York *is* exceptional, I thought. A great city. Sure, it's got its bad points, but the things that're good about it—like right now, being in an empty park with an old buddy on a warm summer night—make up for them. Me on a ranch herding beef cattle? Never.

I could see Freddy was operating on the same wavelength. He told me his family hadn't been back to the Dominican Republic since they took a boat to the States when he was a baby. "And I got no desire to go back," he said. "But my old man's always talking about it. Once a month he threatens to uproot us all and move to Santo Domingo. And y'know why, Ace? He feels like a nobody here. And y'know what else? He felt like a

nobody there, too. That's why he left. He's just fooling
himself, thinking if he was in the D.R. he'd be somebody . . . it keeps him going."

I reached into the bag for more chips. "What does
your old man do?"

"Works nights sweeping out a factory. Never did
learn English. How about yours?"

"Yeah, he speaks English . . . he was born in New
Jersey."

"I meant, what's his job?"

"Telephone repairman. Has been since he married
Mom," I said. "He's constantly crabbing about it."

"Why? He ought to be proud. There're a lot of little
wires in phones, not everybody can fix them. It takes
skill."

For a while neither of us said anything. Freddy's attention seemed to be glued on a plane headed in the
direction of La Guardia Airport and I was concentrating on the silver spire of the Chrysler Building. What an
inspiring sight. Someday I'd write a poem about it:

> *Oh, silver goblet aglow in the night,*
> *Is your bright aura lit from within*
> *Or awashed by a crown of neons?*
> *Are you . . .*

"My brother's gonna be a bum," Freddy said suddenly, jolting me upright.

"Hey! What do you mean? Everybody knows who
Gregory Cruz is! He was one of the all-time greats!
Leader of the famous Marabunta gang!"

"That's not a career, Ace."

"But now he dates a lot of pretty girls."

"That ain't a career either."

"Maybe. But what makes you think he'll be a bum?"

"He's been out of high school two years and all he does is leech bread off the old man. He ain't motivated."

"Ah, give him time," I said. "Something'll interest him. Maybe he'll become an actor like us. He was an extra in a movie once, wasn't he?"

In the dark, Freddy's features looked as heavy and undefined as a face carved out of lava rock. "That's what wrecked him," he said, tearing the cellophane banana-chip bag into a million pieces. "Every night he goes to discos, thinking he'll be discovered. But I seen his film. He ain't got a lick of talent. Nuthin'. And neither have I!"

I was stunned. I couldn't believe Freddy Cruz was talking that way about himself. "You were sensational in *Bound and Gagged!* Marilyn Maroon even said so."

"Ah, cut the bull with me, Ace. I ain't lying to myself. I've gotta think ahead. Plan a career. Decide on something I can be good at."

"So you don't want to work at the Wartzburg. That's it, isn't it? You wanted to meet me here to tell me."

He threw a fistful of cellophane confetti up into the air and plopped back onto the grass. "Whatsa matter with you, man? Don't you hear what I'm saying? I'm scared!" he barked. "I don't want to be a bum or sweep floors. I need that job! Maybe it ain't good enough for you, but I'm taking it. If I'm ever gonna make something of myself, I gotta get out of debt. But I don't want to hold you or the others back from doing what you want. And that's *why* I asked to meet you here . . . *to tell ya!*"

I was so relieved, I collapsed on the grass and let out a two-minute sigh. "I have to take the job too," I said. "If I

don't, my mother's going to make me work in the meat department at Gristede's."

"Heh-heh . . . *you?* The Red Dragon . . . heh-heh . . . grinding chops at Gristede's? Heh-heh."

It was good to hear him laugh. He hardly ever did.

We stayed another hour in the park, shooting the breeze and filling each other in on things we did before we met. He thought I was putting him on when I told him I'd taken tap-dancing lessons when I was in second grade.

"A tough guy like you, Ace?"

"Yeah, and I wore a sailor suit for the recital."

"Know where I spent second grade?" he said.

"In jail?"

"Close to it. I was in the hospital with asthma."

We were on our way out of the park, and I looked down at him as he boosted me up to the top of the fence. "That's sad," I said.

"Yeah, I was a puny little runt. But I learned a couple of good things from it . . . one was how to build up my body."

I dropped to the sidewalk and watched him chin himself to the top bar. His muscles were enough to make Arnold Schwarzenegger eat his heart out. "What was the other thing you learned, Freddy?"

"If I tell you, it's strictly between us, okay? Not even George knows."

"Yeah, sure . . . strictly between us."

He dropped to the sidewalk beside me and looked over his shoulder, making sure that the guy standing on the curb with his dog wasn't in earshot. "I learned to make model airplanes," he whispered. "A nurse got me started with a little Piper Cub. But now? Well, you

name it, I made it. Phantoms, F-14's . . . Thunder
Jets. I got over a hundred models and I'm still making
them. Last night I finished a MiG-27."

"Over a hundred? Jeez! Where do you keep them?"

"In an old pigeon-coop up on my roof."

"Doesn't the rain soak them?"

"Naw. I got 'em all wrapped in heavy plastic."

I was still reeling from our hour of true confessions
when we passed the streetlight down on the corner.
"Ace, ya see these hands?" Freddy asked, backing up to
stretch his fingers up to the light. "They're steady like
surgeons' hands. I could stitch microscopic vessels together, only I ain't smart enough to be a surgeon. So
you know what I'm gonna do?"

"What?" I said, hoping he wouldn't say anything like
"Pick locks."

"I'm gonna become an aviation mechanic!"

Saying good night was tough. Freddy was some guy;
so impressive. I could have walked the streets till sun-
rise, just listening to him tell me more about himself.

"Well, this is it. Time to split," he said when we got to
23rd Street. "See you tomorrow at the Wartzburg."

"Call when you think of a plan to get us up there."

"Right on."

Seven

Five A.M.! I'm always awake at stupid five A.M. when I've got bad problems; big messes I can't handle. I bought my water bed thinking it might soothe my nerves on those occasions, but it doesn't help. Nothing would, short of general anesthesia.

I rolled over and looked at my vent. (My minuscule room doesn't have windows.) This time it was the Piranhas giving me insomnia. Cannibal, the ten-ton goon, in particular. That gorilla doesn't have mere hands. He's got grizzly-bear paws attached to his wrists. For the past hour I'd been picturing them snapping my head off my neck if he ever caught me on his turf.

How were the five of us Falcons going to get in and out of the Bronx *alive* every day? Our days were numbered once the Piranhas found out we'd lied about making a movie in Bermuda with Brooke Shields. Freddy never had come up with a plan. Nobody had. We were all supposed to go home and think one up. Well, here it was. Five A.M. Still no plan.

I got out of bed, turned on my light, and started doing push-ups. Down, up. Down, up. Down, up. Down, *smack!* For a minute I saw stars and sat back on my heels. I'd hit my noggin on the corner of my bookcase. Was that a sign? An omen? I rubbed the lump on my head and stared at my books—eighteen hardcover copies of the Nevada Culhane mysteries. Back in my movie star days, I'd splurged on the entire set. For years Nevada has been my hero. He's the king of detectives, a

cowboy savant, a master of escapes and disguises, the unparalleled lover of beautiful women.

"Speak to me, Nevada," I said. "Give me a plan."

I know that sounds irrational, appealing to a fictitious character for guidance. But I was desperate.

I reached for my copy of *Sinners Be Damned*, closed my eyes, and held my hands on the cover, waiting for a vibration. Nothing happened. I reached for *Ghouls of the Night*. Still nothing.

I glanced at the sixteen titles left on my shelf, trying to recall each story. In one of them, Nevada had strolled through the streets of Hong Kong, disguised to fool a gang of assassins who were out to get him. He'd worn something clever. What was it? And which book was it in?

Was it *The Eighth Deadly Lair?* No, but I was close. It was the sequel, *The Ninth Deadly Lair!* As I yanked it off the shelf the whole Hong Kong scene came back to me. Nevada had dressed as a Chinese woman, carrying his cowboy clothes in a bundle to look like his baby. Eureka! That was it! The plan. We could go to the Bronx as women!

At eight A.M. I heard Dad leave. Forty-five minutes later, Nora left to pick up her dogs. Soon Mom would be on her way to Gristede's. I clasped my hands behind my head and lay back on my pillow, pleased with myself. Now that I'd solved the problem of how to live through the summer, I was able to think of the advantages of working at the Wartzburg. Actually, there was only one: the hours. I'd have time alone in The Pits every day. I could play my stereo, do my . . .

"Horace? You awake?" Mom called.

"Yeah, now I am."

"Are you *sure* your agent got you a job in the Bronx?"

"Yeah, I'm sure."

"Now, you're not just telling me that, are you? Mr. Papadopoulos still needs somebody to work in the meat department and—"

"I got a job, Ma!"

"What time will you be home?"

"About ten . . . like I told you last night."

She sighed. "I wish you'd reconsider. You have no idea how hard it is on a mother, worrying about her only son. The subways are dangerous. Addicts. Muggers . . ."

"I'll be fine, Ma. *Fine!*" Now please leave, I thought.

"Sit next to a cop if you can. Or a nun."

"I'll be with J.D. and George, Ma."

She opened my door a crack. "Please be careful."

"Gimme a massive break . . . I will, I will!"

Five minutes later she was on her way to work wearing her green Gristede's smock. The rest of her clothes —shoes, dresses, skirts, blouses—were all at my disposal. But first I had to make my calls.

Freddy's mother answered at his house, saying, *"Federico no está aquí."*

"Dónde está?" I asked.

"El no me dice nada!"

Slick's mother speaks English with a heavy Italian accent, and she told me he was with Freddy. "It'sa so nice-a you boys gotta jobs-a," she said.

Next I tried J.D. He was still in bed sleeping, and his grandmother told me she'd be happy to wake the bum up. When I had him on the line, I spelled out my plan. "Look, I know it's not ideal," I said, "but it'll work. We'll save our hides . . . the Piranhas would never suspect a tough gang like us Falcons to be dressed up like girls."

He heh-hehed a minute. "There's just one hitch, Ace.

If we all go as girls, they might try to pick us up . . .
grab a feel or somethin'."

"Then *you* think of a better plan," I said.

He heh-hehed again. "You and me could go as a couple. Nobody'd mess with you if you've got a big black
husband with you."

"What about George?"

"Maybe he could go as your sister."

"Great idea," I said.

But George wouldn't buy it. What a grouch! He said
there was no way he'd stoop so low as to ride the subways dressed as my sister, my daughter, my mother, girl
friend, or any other female. "You and J.D. are on your
own, Ace," he said in parting. "I ain't going with you.
I'm getting up to the Wartzburg alone."

Sometimes I think I don't understand George. Then
again, sometimes I think maybe I do. In a book I once
read, it said there are people who would rather die than
give up their principles. They're called tragic heroes,
and George has the makings of becoming one. But not
J.D. and me. We'd give up our principles any day.

It was time to dig through Mom's closet.

I crawled in and took out a pair of strappy spiked high
heels. Crap! I'd never realized she was so little. Size
seven? My feet were that big in kindergarten. I wrestled with them, jamming my toes inside, then thumped
over to the mirror. What a sight. I hiked my zebra p.j.'s
above my knees and looked again. Worse! My hairy legs
nearly made me gag. I could shave them to look more
feminine, but I'd never be able to walk. I had an over-
hang of four inches at the heels.

I tried on flats, wedgies, sandals, and mules. None
came close to fitting. Well, so be it, I thought. I'd have to
ride to the Bronx as one of those tacky women who

wear sneakers with dresses. But first I had to find a
dress.

After a lot of rummaging around in the back of
Mom's closet, I finally found one—a shapeless pink sundress with spaghetti straps. I peeled off my p.j.'s and
tried it on. It was my only hope. Wrong again. Six foot
one in a pink sundress that ends mid-thigh isn't hope.

Bushed and discouraged, I flopped across the folks'
bed, wishing I'd been born in a time when life was
simple. In ancient Rome, for instance. People were so
practical in those days. Short, fat, tall, skinny, or in
between. It didn't matter. One size toga fit them all.
Just get a sheet, wrap it arou— *hey!* What was the matter with me? Mom had something even better than a
toga. Why hadn't I thought of it? Uncle Jake had sent
her a sari from India before he got out of the merchant
marine. She'd given me the Indira Gandhi stamps.

"Hobart, you genius!" I cried, diving for her bureau
drawers. The sari wasn't in any of them.

When I was finished, The Pits looked like it had been
ravaged by a crazed rhino. I cleared out the china cabinet and, in a frenzy, dumped out the contents of the
kitchen junk drawer. Finally, I found the sari stashed
under a pile of napkins in the linen closet. It was still
stored in the original silver box it had come in. I pulled
it out . . . eight yards of gold-bordered aqua silk along
with the instructions on how to put it together. Too bad
I couldn't read Hindi. Well, no sweat. It wouldn't take
me more than three minutes to twirl into it.

Since I had a couple of hours to kill, I showered, ate
breakfast, did my body-building exercises, ate lunch,
watched a quiz show, and fell asleep on the couch during an afternoon soap.

"Did you ever see such a total nincompoop?" The

voice was Nora's. I opened my eyes and saw her and her friend Kelli Constantini looking down at me, faces writhing with disgust. How times had changed, I thought. Six months ago Nora pointed me out to strangers on the street, shouting, "That's my brother . . . Ace Hobart, the famous movie star!"

"Hey, quit staring," I yelled. "And why're you home? I thought you were walking your dogs."

"Finished that hours ago, nincompoop. Now I'm getting all my Barbie stuff to take to Kelli's. C'mon, Kelli."

I dozed off again before they left and didn't wake up till a gong from a quiz show sent me flying off the couch. Holy sh—! I only had fifteen minutes to get into my sari and meet J.D. at the 23rd Street subway.

Twirl, dammit, twirl! Eight yards of silk wasn't as easy to handle as I'd thought. I pinned one end to the armpit of my T-shirt, looped it around my front, spun it over my shoulders, and ended up with five yards hanging over my head. Try again, I told myself. I spun out, then spun back in again, tripping and swearing. Third time around, it looked pretty good, except for that darn end piece.

I didn't have time for a fourth twirl, so I draped the end piece over my head—not bad, actually. It covered my hair. There was still a chunk left and I used that to cover my face like a veil. Then I ran into the bathroom to make a red dot on my forehead with Mom's lipstick.

Five minutes to meet J.D. I jumped into my sneakers, high-tailed it into Nora's room for one of her stuffed animals, grabbed a pillowcase from the linen closet to bundle it in, then squealed into the kitchen for two oranges, scissors, and a roll of Dad's heavy-duty telephone utility tape. In sixty seconds I'd be voluptuous.

Owww! The tape hurt when I adjusted it. Jerk. Why

hadn't I thought of this *before* I draped myself? I snipped off six more two-foot strips and groped around under my sari, plastering these strips diagonally across my torso instead of vertically. Hey! The oranges weren't sagging anymore. Cross Your Heart bras worked! I was ready.

"Wish me luck, Nevada baby," I hollered as I flung open our door.

The orange on my right was a little higher than the one on my left, but I didn't have time to fix it. Out of breath, I kept padding down the stairs, glad I hadn't seen any neighbors and vice versa.

As I hit the second landing I heard voices from below. Nora and her friend Kelli were back. Heart beating like a hot bongo, I pulled my veil higher up my nose, preparing for the moment of truth. Would they recognize me?

We passed each other midway between the first and second floors, them gawking, me with my head lowered, clinging to the shadowy side of the stairway. I was grateful our landlord never installed anything brighter than twenty-five-watt ceiling lights.

"Did you ever see such a *tall* Indian lady?" Nora whispered to Kelli behind my back. Kelli giggled.

The twirps. I might have been a VIP from the UN! I let out a lungful of air when I was out on the sidewalk. If I'd fooled a member of my own family, I could fool anybody.

Well, maybe not. People were staring. The guy going into the cleaners. That woman coming out. Those three kids buying peaches from a street vendor. Hadn't any of them seen tall foreign dignitaries? Or was it my mile-a-minute running walk?

I maintained my speed but narrowed my stride and

concentrated on not being so duckfooted. J.D. was probably waiting for me on the subway platform. I raised the hem of my sari and moved faster. A block from the subway entrance, a drunk with mahogany-colored teeth grinned as I passed him. "You inna marathon?" he said, slurring the words together.

"No speaky dee Eenglais," I said in a high voice. He sure looked familiar. Where'd I seen him?

Going down the steep subway steps, a rotten guy in a rush shoved by me, making me lose my balance. I muttered under my breath as I started to fall, and just then I felt a powerful hand slide under my arm from behind and scoop me upright again.

"Gotta take it easy, lady," said the big, grubby-looking hard-hat type who'd saved me from breaking my neck. He insisted on helping me all the way down and at the bottom he said, "That's a mighty precious package you're carrying," smiling at Nora's stuffed animal rolled up inside a pillowcase. "Is it getting enough air?"

I nodded, hoping he'd leave me alone, but he followed me to the token booth. "How many?" snapped the woman behind the window. I held up two fingers. "Two?" she snapped again. I nodded.

"Listen, don't let her sell you one for the baby . . . you don't need it," said my hard-hat friend.

"Maybe she needs one for her return trip," shouted the woman, taking my money and sliding out two tokens.

"It's people like you, ripping off foreigners, who give this city a bad name," my friend shouted back.

I left the two of them arguing and hurried through the turnstile to the uptown platform. In a crowd of hot, wilted, weary people, I looked for J.D. A guy about his size, in a pin-striped suit and black hat with the brim

turned down over one eye, was leaning against a pillar, twisting the end of his handlebar mustache. J.D. didn't have a mustache, but I sidled over to the guy anyway.

He stared at me under his brim and I stared back over my gold-bordered silk veil. "That you, Ace?" he said, finally.

"J.D.! Where'd you get that mustache?" I whispered.

"Bigelow's Pharmacy on Sixth Avenue . . . it's a paste-on. Like it?"

I nodded and lifted a corner of the pillowcase to let him get a quick peek at Nora's blue monkey. He heh-hehed. "Better keep our little darling's face covered," he said, steering me toward the train when it pulled up.

We had to stand, hanging on to straps, suffocating in the middle of the packed car. The doors slid closed. I nervously took in the sweating, jammed throng to see what kind of expressions we were getting, an interracial couple of unusual height.

Good old New York! Nobody was even looking at us. Not even when I felt sharp yanks at my chest hairs and let out a yelp. Rivulets of sweat had caused the heavy-duty utility tape to come unstuck. My oranges were falling! They dropped down inside my sari, hitting my feet.

The last I saw of them, one was being trampled and the other was rolling down the center of the car.

Eight

We stood at the Wartzburg gates waiting for George. Every so often the watchman came out of his booth, holding an open newspaper, and looked at J.D. and me.

Finally he said, "Whyn't ya move on?" Then he leaned toward us and his mouth dropped open. "Son of a gun, I know who *you* are! You think the Wartzburg is some kind of costume party, you guys? You're supposed to be here working already." He unlocked the gate.

J.D. pointed to the booth. "Can we change in there?"

The watchman nodded and went back to his paper just as a cab pulled up to the gate. We saw George getting out. His face was red as he leaned back in through the open window to pay the driver.

"You and your big ideas!" he yelled at me. "Look at you in that blue-green getup like you're right out of the Taj Mahal. Think I want to go around like that? I took a cab." He marched by the little guardhouse and up the walk.

"Wait a sec; we're going in here to change," J.D. said as he and I squeezed into the guardhouse together.

George didn't stop. "Cost me three bucks to ride that cab from the subway," he threw over his shoulder.

"Tough!" J.D. shouted after him. Then to me he said, "He thinks his feet don't stink. They do."

"What's bothering you?" I said, unwinding myself from the sari.

"George. He never goes along with anybody else.

Always has to be smarter than the rest of us." He helped me drape the sari on a coat hook in the wall.

"Where'll I put the baby?"

J.D. shrugged. I dropped it in the corner and followed him out.

We found George on the porch. Slick and Freddy in white shirts and black ties were serving tea and crumpets to the old people. Pearl Orient and Sir Cecil were sitting at wicker tables on opposite ends of the porch. A few of the residents were in wheelchairs, most in rockers.

"There's the old bag," J.D. said, nudging me. Miss Otterbridge stood supervising teatime in the doorway between what she'd called the veranda and the dining room.

She looked over. I was sure she'd heard him.

"Well, here goes," J.D. said, ignoring George, who was viewing the scene with a suspicious look on his face. "Hello, Miss Otterbridge, here we are!"

She nodded. I smiled my dumb-jerk smile, and she gazed over the white wooden railing at four residents who were in lawn chairs on the grass. The guy we'd seen yesterday on the porch was there, still rocking and talking to himself. Then I noticed that the bushes along the walk had been trimmed. Drastically. They looked like they'd been torpedoed. The box hedge near the house had a crew cut.

J.D. saw it too. He walked over to Miss Otterbridge and said, "How's it goin' . . . with the new gardeners?"

What a dumb question! She was bound to be mad. "Well, it takes a while to learn pruning. Maybe a little experience will help Freddy and Slick," she said mildly.

I'd expected her to snap like a turtle. Instead her eyes misted over and she pointed to the three women and the mumbling old man on the lawn. George pulled himself away from watching the silent, sweaty Freddy pour tea out of a china pot and came over to listen.

"J.D." she said, looking at him, and then at me. "Horace . . . Oh, dear! I've forgotten your name," to George.

"George," he grumbled.

"And George." Her brown hair fluttered in the hot breeze. "I want you to remember something, boys. These people out on the lawn may not seem as . . . well, as *aware* as the others, but it isn't what you think. You have to respect them for what they're doing."

J.D. looked confused. The people were as still as the chairs they were sitting in.

"What *are* they doing?" George said.

"What is normal for their age and condition. They are reliving the best parts of their lives."

We were quiet. "Doesn't that make sense?" she said.

It did to me. I relive making *Bound and Gagged* all the time and being famous and all. That was the best time of *my* life. Miss Otterbridge was looking at me for an answer.

"Oh, oh, yeah! Makes a lot of sense, Miss Otterbridge," I said in a rush, probably not sounding like I meant it, but I really did.

"What a nice resonant voice you have!" she said, looking at me with greater interest. Then her attention went back to the scene on the lawn. "The lady there all in pink played Juliet to perfection years ago. No doubt this summer afternoon, she's recalling the famous matinee when Kaiser Wilhelm came to see her. She was

nineteen, fair as a daffodil . . ." Miss Otterbridge said
dreamily.

The wail of sirens broke the peaceful mood. Out on
the street there were sudden angry shouts and even a
crazy scream as though something fierce had got loose
from the zoo.

"So many fires lately, thousands this year in the Bronx
alone, I read," she said. I looked at J.D., remembering
the punk girls and their matches. "Slick! Over there
now," she called. "Don't forget our guests on the grass,
dear. Such a bright boy!" That was the first time anybody had ever said that about him.

Slick with a tray and a big smile pranced across the
grass as if the old folks were his own private audience.

"Cool it!" I whispered when he passed us, coming
back. He looked at me like I was crazy and kept on
going.

"Some people think older people are laughable,"
Miss Otterbridge said. "Because they're not living in
the present."

"So what's so good about the present?" J.D. said.
"Right?"

"Right!" she said, beaming. I was beginning to like
her a little.

"How 'bout a . . . excuse me. When do we start?"
George interrupted.

"Soon, dear. All of you remember Belva Bithell's
name; she loves it. She's next to the lady in pink. Belva
was in the silent films, one of the 'It' girls, a star known
in every capital, personally by kings and presi-
dents. . . ."

"Calvin Coolidge?" J.D. said, winking at me.

"You know your American history! That's right. The
only thing that detracts from this place is that Ziegfeld

Follies girl, Pearl Orient. She has upset the place!" Miss
Otterbridge looked fierce, but the Wartzburg didn't
look upset to me. Perfectly calm.

Suddenly she squared her shoulders and led us toward the kitchen. "Time for you to get started. Who
likes to pare potatoes?" she said, leading us through all
the old show-biz people on the veranda to a back stairway.

Pearl Orient's eyes snapped open when she saw me.
They were a blur of purple eyeshadow and coal-black
liner. As she caught my glance, she wrinkled up her
nose, "Do you know who I am?" she asked. "I'm the one
who electrocuted John Barrymore in *Wanton Woman!*"

"I heard you were a showgirl . . ."

"*And* a movie star!" she said, sticking out her foot and
tripping me. I fell forward, knocking a teacup out of
somebody's hand. It was the gray-haired twiggy lady I'd
seen the day before.

"Oh, Flora! Did you scald yourself?" her orange-
haired friend asked.

"A little," Flora said, taking the Kleenex I offered and
dabbing tea off her skirt. She looked up. "We haven't
been properly introduced. I'm Flora de Flor and this is
my collaborator, Gayle Godfrey. We're the famous playwrights."

The orange-haired lady smiled at me. "What's your
name, young man?"

"Ace. Ace Hobart."

Just then Miss Otterbridge noticed the spilled tea on
the veranda. "You'll have to clean that up, Freddy. It
wasn't your fault, Horace. Come, we've got to start
preparing dinner."

"Mister Raymond!" she shouted as J.D., George, and I
followed her down the stairs.

We found the cook dozing in a wicker rocker at the foot of the half flight of stairs.

"Wake up this instant!" It was a cry like reveille and the guy shot straight up and looked around.

"Time to start supper!" he cried. "Ha . . . ha, just restin' my eyes."

"Oh, shut up! I know what you're doing or haven't done. George, you missed the tour yesterday. Here are the rules for supper. First, wash your hands thoroughly." She barked out the rest of them while we scrubbed up. On the stove something was bubbling in a caldron. It smelled strange.

"What the heck is cookin'?" J.D. said after she'd left. "Barf!"

Mister Raymond lifted the lid. "One of our favorite foods here. Cow's brain. Want to see it? We've got the whole thing. It's very nourishing, absolutely soft, and extremely digestible." The odor wafted into our appalled faces. I couldn't look.

George licked his lips and said he liked it. After that J.D. and I wouldn't stand near him while we peeled potatoes.

"I like other parts, too," he said evilly. I wasn't sure whether to believe him or not, and I didn't ask him what parts either.

The menu that night was this. *Melon balls.* (Done by J.D.) He scooped those near the sink while Slick and Freddy rinsed off the tea dishes and put them in the dishwasher. Slick picked some of the orange-and-green balls out of the colander and started flipping them at everybody until Mister Raymond grabbed his neck and threatened to push his head under the faucet. (Later

when we ate our supper after everybody else, I noticed that some of the melon balls tasted like soap bubbles.)

Or sweat. Freddy sweated the whole time he was in the kitchen. He lost about five pounds, I bet. That smell and the cooking odors amounted to quite a lot. I had to keep swallowing and thinking of green grass and sucking ice cubes.

The menu. Next course was the main. Or the *entree! Creamed mashed potatoes.* (I did those.) *Creamed brain.* (George sliced it up and it slid all over the cutting board like it was still alive.) And one thing not creamed. *Baby peas.*

At six o'clock everything was ready to be served. Time, also, for Freddy and Slick to get off work, which they did in a hurry without anybody reminding them. They didn't even say good-bye to George, J.D., and me. We had three hours to go and carried loaded trays upstairs.

All four of those people who were reliving the best parts of their lives also turned out to be reliving their baby days. Each of them had to be spoon-fed. And J.D. and I each had to feed *two* of them! I drew Juliet in pink, and old, mumbling Whar Ma Bleedin' From for my first time.

"Time to eat!" I begged. "Here's dinner, yum, yum, yum, good for you. Come on!" I said to Juliet. Her mouth clamped shut. "Come on, please!"

Miss Otterbridge got suspicious and came over. When she saw that exactly none of that delicious food had disappeared off either plate, she grabbed the spoons out of my hands and put one in each of her own. "Like this!" she whispered.

"Attention! Open up. Open your mouths! Now!" she

commanded. Everybody in the whole place could hear her. J.D. started to giggle.

Juliet and Whar Ma Bleedin' From just stared.

"No teevee!" she shouted.

Both their mouths fell open simultaneously. She shoveled the food in until they closed them again and swallowed. She said later, it would have been a crime for her to let them starve.

When dessert finally came, it felt about midnight. I was beat. George was limping from where Pearl Orient had kicked his shins for not asking if she wanted second helpings. Gayle Godfrey was trying to change seats with Flora de Flor so she could be next to Sir Cecil, but Flora wouldn't.

Dessert was *Cream custard.* They said that we could eat now, after everybody else had left the dining room. There was enough left over to feed the poor people of the Bronx and some in Queens. We didn't make a dent in it; I'd rather have had runny rice and *colorados* at La Bombola China Grande. Only we could never eat there again, except maybe in disguise.

"Come on, you're falling asleep on the job! Get those pots and pans *clean!"* said Mister Raymond. It was long past nine o'clock when the three of us finished up and dragged ourselves down the walk to the guardhouse to get our disguises.

"Oh, by the way, I've got an audition tomorrow," George said. "It's nice to know you can be excus—"

"Wait a minute! You're not leaving *me* and *Ace* to do all that work," J.D. shouted.

"Well . . ." George shrugged as we went through the gates toward the subway. J.D. and I didn't bother to put on our getups. It was dark and we figured luck

would keep us from getting seen tonight if we'd been seen yesterday. The odds, statistics, et cetera . . .

"You *really* got an audition, George?" J.D. said, sounding jealous.

"They want me to play King Kong on top of the Empire State Building. Think I'll take it. It'll be a lot easier than this job," he said.

We looked at him slowly. He was kidding! We were too tired to laugh, but at least I felt a little better about him than I had all day.

Nine

"You could quit, Horace. Mr. Papadopoulos still hasn't found anybody to work in the meat department," Mom said, following me from the fridge to the living room while I ate a jar of pickled herrings. "He'd hire you in a minute. I know he would."

"Look! For the last time, Ma! I'm not quitting. Just because there've been a couple of little fires in the Bronx . . ."

"Not a couple, Horace! And not little! *And stop dripping that stuff on the couch.* . . ."

The scene I'm describing took place two weeks after the Falcons and I started working at the Wartzburg. Mom was a wreck every day, worrying about me going up there. And she never stopped talking about it. . . .

"You have no idea how awful it is, Horace. And with those terrible arsonists . . ."

Nora looked away from her TV program. "What're arsonists?"

"Vicious criminals who set fires," Mom said, holding up the headlines of the morning paper. "See? Another building burned down in the Bronx. The third one this week."

I knew. I'd been keeping track. But I wasn't taking the fires personally like she was. My biggest concern, other than my dishpan hands, was us Falcons going to and from work without the Piranhas spotting us. So far we hadn't crossed paths since our meeting at La Bombola China Grande. After four days on the job I'd

felt safe enough to stop wearing my sari. And just yesterday old George had joked that maybe the Piranhas
had been farmed out to some rich families in the coun-
try as part of the Fresh Air Fund.

"Horace is probably the one setting fires," said Nora.

Mom dropped the newspaper. "Nora! For shame!
Horace is a good boy. And you know how he hates
heat."

Nora shrugged. "Then who *is* setting the fires?"

Good question. And it's just what George, J.D., and I
talked about on the way up to the Bronx the next afternoon. But it wasn't until later that we got the real clue
as to who was setting some of those fires.

It was hot. Ninety-seven degrees! When we got to the
Wartzburg, there were sprinklers all over the lawn,
squirting the wilted grass. I wished I could take my
clothes off like a little kid and run through them, squish-
ing my toes in the wet grass.

We found Miss Otterbridge under the big ceiling fan
in the kitchen. She was talking very seriously to Freddy
and Slick. "I'm glad you're here; there's been a crisis,"
she said, opening an ice tray. "Mister Raymond, who's
never missed a day on the job, has suffered heat prostra-
tion."

It wasn't from standing over a hot stove, she said.
He'd passed out in the little garden outside, cultivating
herbs for his salads. Poor old Bunion Feet! He was upstairs in bed with a headache, fever, and nausea. Miss
Otterbridge was filling an icepack for him. Not only
could he not do the cooking, but he wasn't able to go to
the market as he did every day for fresh fruits and
vegetables. The old folks were spoiled!

"So I have to rely on you boys to fill the gap. Freddy
and Slick, you're on double shift," she said, screwing the

cap on the rubber pack. "You can help George, J.D., and Horace do the shopping. And then together we'll fix dinner. For the extra work, you'll all get double wages. Are you willing?"

Double wages? It was a silly question, but Slick, who'd been sucking an ice cube, put it into his hand and said, "Where's the market, far from here?" Then he slapped the cube back in his mouth.

I wasn't worried about the distance, but whether the way was paved with punk rockers.

"Just twenty blocks, in the Italian neighborhood, where the food is lovely," she said.

Fifteen minutes later, with a grocery list as long as a Piranha's arm and two hundred dollars divided up and stashed in our shoes, we were on our way across the dangerous reaches of the Bronx. J.D. was in the lead as lookout; Slick brought up the rear as guard. George had put himself in charge of the expedition to the Bellissimo Mercato by snatching the list when Miss Otterbridge extended her hand.

We reached the market and joined the jostling crowd of shoppers, who were mostly housewives. Inside the plain brick building were dozens of stalls and booths full of big, beautiful fruits and vegetables. All colors and all kinds! Vendors were hawking sausages, pastas, cheeses, and breads from the counters on the sides. There were barrels of olives and pickles and nuts. It smelled so good, my mouth watered.

"Fifteen melons, honeydew. You get those, Slick," George commanded. "J.D., pick up ten pounds of red ripe tomatoes. I'll get potatoes for the potato salad, cabbage for the slaw."

"How do I know which of these is ripe?" Slick said next to a pale green melon mountain.

"Squeeze 'em and smell 'em," Freddy barked. "Like Miss Otterbridge said."

"Think I know how to do that!" Slick snapped.

"Do it anyway!"

Freddy and I checked out corn on the cob that had *just* been flown in from Georgia, the vendor said. I wondered how the wiggling worm I found in the first ear had liked the flight.

"Boy, it's good we don't have to pick up the meat, too," J.D. said after we'd spent way over an hour buying the food. We were in a store as fragrant as a pizza parlor. Hanging above us was a wall-to-wall ceiling of sausages. Freddy was getting the bread and we all bought a few little snacks for ourselves.

Then we started back, toting thirteen loaded bags between us. All except Slick. He'd been sent ahead to patrol for the Piranhas. Next thing we knew, we'd lost him! Then J.D. gasped and pointed out that behind us were not two but *four* ugly punk girls. I turned and spotted them through the leafy crowns of celery sticking out of one of my heavy bags.

"Are they the ones you saw?" George whispered.

"Uh-uh!" I said. "No!" These punks had shaved heads and were pale as boiled chickens. Like newborn birds! As soon as we stopped and turned, they disappeared in the crowds. Or hid.

Just then one of J.D.'s bags slipped and fell on the street, spilling peppers, lemons, and lettuce all over his shoes. That's when we found Slick again. He was under a shady awning, eating a Popsicle and talking to the black-eyed Italian beauty with the ice-cream cart. She had little sweat bubbles above her full lips, I noticed. Freddy didn't blow his top at Slick. Instead, he just set

his bags down on the hot cement and bent over to retrieve the stuff J.D. had dropped.

"Hurry up!" muttered George, his face red. "We gotta get outta here before those Amazons see where we're goin'. You guys weren't kidding. Crap! They looked mean. Come *on*, Slick!"

We hustled.

With Miss Otterbridge's help, we unloaded, washed, prepared the salads, and then arranged the fruits, the bread, the cold chicken delivered from the deli, and the eggs and corn we'd boiled in the kitchen, on thirty-five trays for supper. It took endless hours. When we finally served the residents on the veranda, where there was a tiny breeze, we were almost an hour late. Except for Pearl, the old folks were so mad, they wouldn't eat. After all that time and work, we had to throw out half the food we'd bought and fixed! Although Mister Raymond was feeling better now, Miss Otterbridge wouldn't let him come down into the heat of the kitchen. By ten, when we'd finished running the dishwashers, it was nuclear meltdown in there.

What a relief when the five of us shuffled out the Wartzburg's gates a little later!

"The sidewalk's the same temp as human skin. Whew!" George yelled over the sounds of sirens and people yelling somewhere not too far away.

"Something stinks!" Slick said, sniffing the air.

I thought I smelled smoke, and wondered how the old folks slept through the incessant noise of the fire engines.

"Something's burning," Slick said, stopping. He was the only one of us who looked cool. Before leaving, he'd stuck his head under the faucet and soaked it. Then

he'd splashed Brut all over himself. He carries that instead of Neo-Synephrine now.

You could see smoke, but not where it was coming from. When we turned the corner, we ran smack into a fire. It wasn't in a building. It was a huge bonfire in a flaming oil drum in the middle of the dark street.

"Look out!" said George.

Gangs of kids were milling about. Flames leapt into the air and cracked like fireworks. Through the thick smoke I saw dozens of sticks stuck into the barrel. Near it a hydrant was open, water gushing across the street, but nowhere near the thirsty flames. Where were the fire engines? The heat was intense. The kids were yelling and moving around and suddenly, before we could decide what to do, a female voice screamed, *"Falcons!"*

The punk rockers. The bonfire flared, and suddenly we were face-to-face with Flame and Ember. And a whole lot of others.

Ember screamed, "Movie stars! Let's set 'em on fire!"

Then Flame raised her big arm in the air. She was holding a red-hot stick pulled from the fire. Other punks grabbed sticks out of the flaming drum and came toward us.

"Let's get outta here!" Slick said, turning and leaping toward the corner we'd come from. Freddy followed, and when he moved, we all went.

The gang of screaming pyromaniacs fell in behind us, chasing us down the street with sticks raised. They chanted, "Get 'em, get 'em!"

Flame was closing in behind me. I caught the sight of the stick with its red-hot point. My shoes pounded the sidewalk. She hit me with the poker and I felt the heat through my jeans. "Get away, you jerk!" I yelled at her.

I passed Slick and Freddy, then George shot ahead,

careening around a trash can, heading toward the subway station. I knocked the trash can into the road behind me. Suddenly George turned right, toward the
open door of the Bronx Model Youth League. He ran
inside, and the rest of us followed him in like the tail of a
cracked whip.

Outside, the crowd yelled, beating on the door. He
locked it from inside, flipping the bolt, sliding the chain.
Then there were sirens, cop cars, bright searchlights on
the street. The crowd was pulling away from us, dis-
persing, disappearing into the night.

We caught our breath in the grubby BMYL lounge. It
was air-conditioned, but not cool, just better than the
steaming streets outside. At the desk a small old man
was dozing. When we came in, he'd looked up without
saying anything. Now he seemed asleep again.

George pointed at a stack of pamphlets on the radia-
tor near the door and a plaque that said A PERSONAL
MESSAGE FOR YOU FROM IRIS WELCH.

"She's the woman who tried to push Kool-Aid and
crackers on me the first day we were up here," he said.

J.D. picked up a pamphlet and thumbed through it.
"Guess we're safe here; those freaks can't be model
youth," he said.

"I think they're all gone," I said, looking at the hole
burned in my pants. The *Oui!* symbol was ruined.

"Think it's safe to go?" Slick said.

"Yeah," J.D. said, putting down the pamphlet. "Let's
get our singed butts outta the Bronx."

We took his advice and left, flying down the subway
station steps and hopping the first train home.

Ten

Arson, along with local murders, holdups, and nursing-home scandals, was a taboo subject at the Wartzburg. Miss Otterbridge had said as much after the first bad fire in the neighborhood. But when the building *across the street* went up in flames, the *same hot night* the pyromaniacs chased us, she couldn't keep the residents from feeling upset. Pearl, she told us when we arrived the next day, had needed a tranquilizer.

To reassure and comfort everyone, she'd planned a fire drill. All of us on the staff were told exactly what to do. It was planned for late afternoon after tea.

Teatime had a real zing to it that afternoon, for the waiters and gardeners, that is. We whisked in and out of the sun-room, where tea was being served, filling cups, slicing lemons, mopping up spills, and brushing away cookie crumbs as if we had high-voltage currents running through us.

"Whar's the fire?" said old Whar Ma Bleedin' From.

I gently tugged his paper napkin out of the collar of his shirt and added it to the things on my take-away cart.

"Oh, there's no fire," I said. "We're just running a little late today, is all."

He rocked a few times and looked up at me. "Is my ear bleedin'?"

"No, it's fine," I said.

"An Apache Injun shot me with an arrow," he said, rocking again.

"Doesn't show," I said.

That was about the extent of the talking going on, except, of course, among the employees.

"Whaddya say, Ace? Think we ought to liven everybody up a bit before the drill?" George asked me while we were wiping the tea tables. "If we don't, we're gonna end up toting them all out of here."

I looked over at two-ton Pearl, flaked out across a couch in her orange satin housecoat. Just one of her whiskey-barrel legs would break my back. "Good idea, George. How'll we do it?"

"Maybe I can talk PeeWee into playing some ragtime," he said.

No sooner was PeeWee sitting at the piano than the alarm went off. "Okay, men. Time for action," Freddy called after the first bong.

Slick dropped his sponge, J.D. sprinted to the aid of Juliet in pink, I stared at Pearl Orient, dozing tranquilly, and George made a beeline for one of the old vaudeville actors.

Within seconds the staff nurses, housekeepers, Mister Raymond, and Alfonso, the handyman, appeared in the sun-room, wearing colored armbands Miss Otterbridge had issued us. They were ready to help us with the mass exodus.

"Hey! What's going on?" Pearl asked when I shook her arm and told her to get off the couch.

"No cause for alarm . . . we're just having a fire drill," I said.

"Then wake me when it's over."

"No, really, Miss Orient. You've got to get up . . . you have to," I pleaded. "Miss Otterbridge is timing

this. She wants to make sure that all the residents can be led to safety in the event of a *real* fire."

Pearl yawned, patting her mouth. "Why should I listen to old Snootface? Think she ever listens to me? I told her over and over that there's a gang of girl arsonists here in the Bronx."

"You *know* about them!"

"That's right, sonny. Old Snootface wants them to burn us in our beds."

"Where'd you hear about those girls?" I whispered.

"Where do you think?" she snapped. "From Louie."

"Louie who? A cop?"

"No, Louie the fryman at La Bombola China Grande . . . he knows everything!"

I grabbed one arm, then the other, trying to hoist her off the couch, but she kept wrestling away from me. Next I grabbed for her middle. "Upsy-daisy," I said, unable to budge her. *Where were my assistants? Why weren't they helping me?*

I was sure Pearl and I were the only ones left in the sun-room. Then I looked up and saw that hardly anybody else had gone. Two staff nurses had a small band of residents near the door, and George and the handyman were rounding up another one in the middle of the room.

"Look, this is a fire drill—d-r-i-l-l—happening in the *present,*" somebody in J.D.'s red squad was saying to old Whar Ma Bleedin' From sitting in his green rocker. "Huh? No, you're *not* bleeding."

"And we're only giving you till the count of five to get up," J.D. said. "One, two . . ."

Slick was arguing with Flora and Gayle, the playwrights, over which of the three of them was going to push Sir Cecil's wheelchair.

"Don't forget *I've* known him over fifty years," said one.

"Don't forget he was engaged to *me,*" said the other.

"Don't forget *I'm* the one wearing the purple armband," said Slick.

I couldn't believe my eyes! While they were still arguing, Sir Cecil got up, without a word, and walked away from his wheelchair. That faker! His legs worked as well as mine did. ". . . four . . . four and a quarter . . . four and a half," J.D. was counting, "four and three quarters . . ."

I finally spotted Jacqueline, a beautiful candy-striper from the Housekeeping Department, with PeeWee in tow. "Have you seen Leslie? She's on my squad," I called.

Jacqueline nodded in the direction of the window. I looked over and saw Leslie, arm in arm with Belva Bithell, taking teeny millimeter-a-minute steps. At that rate, it was going to take them an hour just to cross the rug.

So what was I going to do with Pearl Orient? What would Nevada Culhane do in my predicament? Bribe her, probably. How, though? How does anyone bribe a two-ton, eighty-year-old femme fatale with aqua eyelids and platinum spit curls?

"I know somebody who thinks you're the sexiest dish he's ever seen," I said, telling her the first thing that came to me.

Pearl smoothed one of her rumpled ringlets. "All men think I'm sexy."

"But this guy is extremely rich and handsome . . . in fact, he's a sheik," I lied. "He rode camels before he bought his jet."

"Ohh? Anybody I know?"

"Maybe. But I won't tell you who he is unless you follow me out of the Wartzburg," I said.

My tactic worked. Pearl stayed glued to my elbow all the way down the stairs, out the front door, across the porch, and down to the lawn. "Okay, sonny. Tell me now. What's his name? Is he married? Have I ever met him?" she said as we lined up behind the nurses and their group.

"Shhhhh. Later. We can't talk during a fire drill," I said.

She pinched a tender little fold of skin under my arm so hard, the pain shot into my chest. "What's his *name,* sonny?"

"Ewwww . . . ouch! It's Sheik Ali Cous-Cous of Marrakech."

"Will you bring him here to meet me?"

"Owww . . . agh! Yes, yes . . . I'll bring him. Ouch!"

"Next week?"

"Aghhh . . . Aghhhh!" The pain was searing my whole upper torso. All I could do was nod.

"Don't forget!"

She let go and I rubbed my arm, rocking, chewing my lip, trying not to black out. I'd had no idea people her age could be so vicious, so nasty. So strong.

"There's old Snootface," she said.

I looked up at Miss Otterbridge, standing on the porch, timing the fire drill with a stopwatch. Why was she acting so pleased? It had taken us nearly forty-five minutes. And some people were still in there.

"Excellent! Bravo!" she cheered as Belva Bithell came out the door on Leslie's arm, bowing like she was taking a curtain call.

Straggling behind them was J.D.'s red squad. They'd

lifted the old guy out of his green rocker and carried him downstairs.

Miss Otterbridge shouted into a megaphone, "Now that we're all assembled, I'd like to congratulate each and every one of you! This has been a most satisfying exercise. Most efficient! It has proven beyond a shadow of a doubt that we have nothing to fear . . . not even fear of fire itself. We did it! And we can do it again!"

George was standing with his group a few feet away from me, grinning as he listened. When our eyes met, he gave me the A-OK sign. "Freud could've learned a few lessons from her, huh, Ace?"

"Yeah . . . right," I said, massaging my throbbing arm.

As her speech shifted into a special announcement, I noticed we'd attracted a crowd of onlookers from the street. Better than fifty people were staring in at us from the gates—men in cutoffs, women and babies, kids shooting each other with water pistols. Then I thought I saw . . . no, couldn't be. Stab and Cannibal near the burned-out building across the street with those punk girls?

"The Actors Guild has sent us complimentary tickets to the Old Timers Game at Yankee Stadium, this Saturday," Miss Otterbridge's voice boomed out across the yard. "Anybody interested in going may sign up in my office immediately after this fire drill."

I looked back over my shoulder at the crowd. Naw, they weren't there. Me and my old hyperactive imagination.

Women!

Raven, my best girl, was always too busy to see me.

Jacqueline, the pretty housekeeper, said she was involved in a "meaningful" relationship with her drama coach, whatever that meant. Nora was nagging me to pay back the nine bucks I'd borrowed from her dog money—*plus* eighteen percent interest! And Mom was having a fit because I'd signed up for the Yankee game on Saturday. She thought I was lying. ("Don't tell *me* stories about chaperoning the old folks, Horace! You're cutting work to go, aren't you?")

But that fiend, Pearl Orient, took the cake. She was almost worse than those punk rockers who tried to singe our butts.

Every day at work she'd pinch the sore bruise she'd ground into my arm, reminding me of my promise to introduce her to Sheik Ali Cous-Cous. I couldn't escape her. Finally I came right out and confessed that I'd lied. "You *lied?*" Her eyes went all out of focus and she slammed me one in my gut, screaming, "Don't you ever, ever, *ever* lie to me again!"

But relief was in sight. My buddies, the Falcons, and I were getting together for breakfast on Saturday. The five of us hadn't had a good time in weeks. We agreed to meet at Mario's Pizzeria, our old hangout near Kennedy High in Manhattan, to talk and gorge ourselves with junk food. When I got there, J.D., George, and Freddy were already sitting in a booth, waiting for me.

"Just like old times, huh, Ace?" Freddy said, sliding over so I could sit next to him.

He meant our black leather Falcon jackets. "Yeah, sure is," I said, unzipping mine. It was a humid, eighty-five degrees, but we'd worn them out of nostalgia.

"Whaddya want, Ace? The works?" said J.D. "Pepperoni, sausages, anchovies, garlic, peppers, mushrooms, onions . . ."

"Don't forget fries," said Freddy.

"And jelly donuts," said George.

"Aren't we waiting for Slick?" I asked.

The three of them shot each other such dark looks, I was sure there'd been a death in Slick's family.

"He ain't coming," Freddy said.

"Why? What's happened? Was it his grandmother?"

"You tell him," J.D. said to George.

"You tell him," George said to Freddy.

"Don't matter who tells him as long as he's told," Freddy said.

"Well, somebody tell me!"

Freddy shrugged and looked at me. "It's like this, Ace. Slick's changed . . . he ain't the same as he was. He's been hanging out with that dancin' teacher at the health club. You know, the one who taught him plee-ays? And now he thinks he's Mr. Fancy Pants."

"Tell Ace where your brother's been seeing them," said George.

"I'm gettin' to that," said Freddy. He brushed a gummy chunk of mushroom off the table and looked at me again. "Last night he was cuttin' up in Auntie Maim's disco in a lavender tank top and white stretch pants that hugged his buns."

All I'd noticed was that Slick's grooming had improved. He'd been reeking of after-shave and hadn't

been spitting or wiping his nose with a gray rag, lately.
But I had no idea it was this serious.

"He's also been foolin' around on the job, not doin'
his share," said George.

"Like letting Freddy wash all the tea dishes," said
J.D.

"How long's this been going on?" I asked.

"For two weeks!" said Freddy.

"And you've been letting him get away with it?"

"Look, Ace! The dope's my friend . . . I can't keep
laying him out every day!"

"You mean you *beat* him *up?*"

Freddy looked like he was going to be sick and
started to stand, but George reached across the table,
pushing him down again. "Damn . . . quit worrying!
If you killed him, his mother woulda told you."

"Maybe I should call her," said Freddy.

"You called three times already!"

"But you shoulda seen his face, George. All twisted
. . ." Freddy smooshed his nose and stretched the corner of his mouth to his ear, demonstrating. "He looked
like a leftover eggplant lyin' there."

"Jeez . . . lying where?" I asked.

"On the stoop of his building," said J.D.

"Since when?"

"Since eight. That's why he ain't eating breakfast
with us."

Customers were beginning to swarm into the pizzeria, and Mario, the one-man operator with the bald,
sweat-glazed head, looked over at our booth like he was
getting annoyed. "You celebrities ever gonna place
your order?" he hollered.

"We'll have a large pie with the works, a basket of

fries, a dozen jelly donuts, and five, I mean *four,* Cokes," J.D. called.

We ate in morbid silence, except that now and again Freddy would sink his face in his hands and say, "I shouldn't've hit him so hard," and George would say, "Look, it ain't your fault, Freddy!"

Getting together wasn't much fun with Slick missing, but all in all it didn't affect our appetites. After the food at the Wartzburg, we were starving for junk. When we finished our first order, we ordered a calzone and four more sodas.

Mario was Mr. Smileypuss when he came over to add up our check. "Was a little surprised to see you," he said. "Just yesterday somebody was in, saying he'd heard you were making another movie and had I heard about it. I said I hadn't and he said it was on location somewhere . . . Bermuda, I think it was."

"We didn't like our parts, so we quit," I said.

"Ace is only joking," George said, kicking me under the table. "We'll be in Bermuda all summer. We just flew home for the weekend, is all."

"Making real big bucks, huh?"

"Yeah, real big bucks. Five thou a week." George tilted his glass, shaking out an ice cube. "By the way, Mario . . . who was this guy who told you about the movie? MGM's been keeping it secret. Nobody's supposed to know."

Except the Piranhas, I suddenly realized.

"Oh, some eight-foot lunk with hands like ham hocks. Not a regular customer."

George crunched his ice. "Sounds like a spy from the Stab Evans Talent Agency," he said.

"Anybody with him?" asked Freddy.

"Yeah, he had these two really"—Mario's eyes swiv-

eled to see if any customers were in earshot—"ugly girls. And I mean *really* ugly! Shaved heads, and tattoos. Look like they'd eat their young for appetizers."

"Stab Evans Talent Scouts, all right," said J.D.

We all nodded.

"Funny, though, that they'd be in here looking for you if they thought you was in Bermuda," Mario said.

That's show biz, we said. Then we paid our bill, leaving him to figure out the mystery. We had it figured. The girls were the bald birds who'd followed us the day we went to the market for Miss Otterbridge.

When we got out to the street, Freddy looked at his watch. "I'd better be heading up to the Wartzburg. You guys are coming at noon today?"

The rest of us nodded.

"It ain't safe going up there in your Falcon jacket," J.D. said. "Better take it off and wear a disguise."

"Don't have time for one," said Freddy.

J.D. reached into his pocket and handed him the fake mustache he'd been carrying in case of an emergency. "You got time for this."

The mustache didn't have much stickum stuff left on it, but Freddy was still able to press it in place over his lip. "Now gimme your jacket," said J.D.

"How do I look?" said Freddy.

"Like that Mexican guy, Viva Zapata," George said, but Freddy didn't laugh.

We walked him two blocks to the nearest subway and watched him go down the steps alone. By himself, he didn't give the impression of being a big, tough gang leader. I think he was sorrier than ever he'd beat up Slick.

"See you later," I called.

"Yeah, and who knows? Maybe Slick'll be okay to come to the Yankee game later," called J.D.

Freddy looked back at us. "Don't count on it."

Twelve

George relented. "Okay! I'll go to the Bronx in disguise. But just this once. And *only* as a bag lady."

Then J.D. said that since Freddy had his mustache, maybe he ought to go as a bag lady too.

Then I decided it might look suspicious for a UN delegate in a silk sari to accompany two bag ladies, so we went as three bag ladies.

For seventy-five cents we got most of the ratty used clothing we needed at the Salvation Army headquarters on 14th Street. The other stuff—paper shopping bags, a torn rain slicker, and a few filthy odds and ends —came from trash cans.

Where to put it all on was our big problem. None of us could go home on Saturday, not with our families around. And due to crime the subways' public rest rooms had been shut down.

"Guess we'd better head up to Forty-second Street and use the men's room at Grand Central," J.D. said.

About thirty unhealthy-looking old men were lined up ten-deep, waiting for vacant stalls, when we got there.

"If we blow this and the Piranhas recognize us, we're *dead!*" George said as we stood in line. "We gotta look authentic. So layer. Put on everything in your bags."

I did: first my torn, runny Supp-Hose, then dirty gray tube socks, a pair of decayed leather slippers, then a huge grungy sack dress topped by two diseased-looking

sweaters, then something so grungy I couldn't tell what
it was. Maybe a horse blanket.

Once my red cotton kerchief was tied under my chin,
I was set. I grabbed my shopping bags and waddled out
of my stall, not looking right or left. "Hey! Can'tcha
read? This is a *men's room!*" a guy shouted as he was
going in and I was coming out.

"Hey! What's goin' on? Here comes another one,"
somebody else shouted as J.D. tried sneaking out of his
stall, looking like a walking rummage sale.

"What're these hags havin'? A convention?" another
guy shouted.

"Ya ask me, it's those women's libbers what's behind
this," came another voice.

"Uncle Sam oughta draft every last one of them."

J.D. and I beat it out of the men's room fast and found
George waiting for us, over by the shoeshine stand, in a
moth-eaten tweed skirt and a torn yellow rain slicker.
"Not bad . . . not bad at all," he said when he saw us.

He looked pretty good himself once he pulled his
stocking cap over his eyebrows. But the rancid gray
scarf he'd wound around his neck nearly made me sick.

"Maybe you shouldn't wear that," I said. "It might
give you hepatitis."

"Or something worse," J.D. added.

"Look! I ain't exactly planning on eating it," George
said.

In the subway, nobody came near us. We had the
whole middle section of seats on the left to ourselves.

By then I was starved. I couldn't take my eyes off the
pretzel that a little kid sitting on his mother's lap, directly across from me, was eating. Jeez, it looked good.
One of those fresh-baked chewy ones with rock salt.
Every time he took a bite, my mouth watered.

Finally his mother caught me staring, picked the kid up, and moved to another seat. But when the train screeched into the 125th Street station, she back-tracked to come by me on her way out the door.

"Buy yourself something to eat," she said, slipping a dollar bill in my hand. "You look hungry."

"Jeez, thanks! I am. But I really shouldn't take—"

George's elbow whammed my side. "Shut up, Ace!"

I stuffed the dollar in my sock and looked at him. Man, he was acting peculiar. Sort of twitchy.

"Relax. Everything's gonna be okay," I whispered.

He scratched his thigh and glared at me like he was the Grim Reaper. "Drop dead!" he said.

When we got out at our stop on 170th Street, he was carrying on like a frenzied madman. He didn't even wait for the light on the corner. He hopped from one foot to the other, violently clawing away under his slicker, then he grabbed his bags and took off, weaving through the oncoming traffic. J.D. and I ran after him, dodging the cars honking at us.

"Hey, George . . . cool it, man," J.D. said when we caught up. "We got six minutes to get to the Wartzburg, okay?"

"And there's not a sign of Piranhas or punks anywhere," I said.

George's head jutted forward. "Dammit, can't you see?" he shrieked. "It's my skirt! It's got bugs in it!"

Men, women, kids, dogs, two white-robed Muslims, a peddler selling ties, and a couple holding hands all moved from the center of the pavement like the Red Sea parting for Moses as we raced for the Wartzburg.

I was sure my body temperature had hit 110 under my horse blanket. My mouth was parched. Up the street, I eyed a guy in a sombrero hawking slices of

watermelon from the trunk of his beat-up Dodge Dart.
I slowed down. George and J.D. could keep running
and collapse if they wanted, but I was stopping to buy
myself a nice cool juicy wedge of watermelon.

I dropped my bags on the curb, held up my dollar
bill, and panted to the hawker, "Gimme a—" then
choked. Cannibal and Stab Evans! Sitting right there
eating watermelon, spitting their seeds in the gutter.

I snatched my bags just as Cannibal looked up and
saw me. "Hey, Stab," he said with pink juice rolling
down his chin. "Don't we know her from somewheres?"

I've never run faster. My guess is, I did three blocks in
a little better than twenty-five seconds. "Gate's unlocked," a familiar voice yelled as I streaked up to the
Wartzburg. "Just push it open."

I crashed through it with my shoulder and went tum-
bling over my bags as I hit the inside walk. For a minute
I lay there in a heap, trying to catch my breath, then I
saw the watchman sitting in a lawn chair, sighing.

"The other two freaks are in there," he said, nodding
toward the guardhouse.

I was greeted by a wild flurry of flying clothes when I
opened the door. "Jeez, look at my legs! Look at 'em!"
George was screaming.

J.D. and I bent down to examine them. From the
knees on up they were a mass of red, comma-shaped
welts, thick as slugs. "I think they're hives," I said.

"Yeah, I know . . . it's the wool, the wool in the skirt!
I forgot I'm allergic to wool!"

J.D. started to pull on his pants. "Next time maybe
you'd better wear a slip, George."

It was 12:04 when we walked into the Wartzburg, dressed for the ball game.

Miss Otterbridge had everybody who was going lined up in pairs in the parlor, giving them last-minute instructions on our "buddy system." When she was finished, she came over to George, J.D., and me, shaking her head. "It's just dreadful about poor Slick," she said. "Absolutely dreadful."

"He's *here?*" I asked.

"Oh, no, of course not. He was knocked unconscious!"

"You mean Freddy *told you* what happened?" said George.

"Imagine!" she said. "A truck just backed onto the sidewalk and hit Slick."

J.D. and I shook our heads. "Poor Slick."

"But don't you worry, Miss Otterbridge," said George. "When the game's over, we're gonna go light candles for him."

"I'd appreciate it if you lit one for me, too," she said. Then, still looking concerned, she reached into her pocket and handed me a message that read: *Ace—call your mother immediately. It's urgent.*

"Go ahead, dear. Use the phone in my office."

Good old Ma, I thought as I sat in Miss Otterbridge's swivel chair, dialing home. She's found out I wasn't lying about chaperoning the residents to the game. And now she wants to apologize.

"Hi, Ma . . . it's me," I said when she answered.

"Horace Hobart, how could you?" she screeched in my ear. "With all our bills, how could you do this? *How?"*

"Do what?"

"Order that hanging-upside-down thing and . . ."

"Ma, I'm sorry. I forgot to canc—"

". . . so I open the invoice," she was still screeching, "and what do I see? That you owe a balance of a hundred . . ."

"Ma, listen. Don't worry. I'll—"

"Don't worry? You have the nerve to tell me that, Horace? To your mother who scrimps and saves and buys her clothes in bargain basements? Who sits up nights clipping coupons? Who never leaves a room without turning the lights out? Never . . . *ohhhh,* you used to be such a nice boy, Horace," she said. "Considerate. Helpful. And you know what changed you? *Being in that movie!* And fancying yourself a hotshot movie star! *You* had to get a water bed . . . and sleep in silk pajamas! *And now, here you are"*—she was back to screeching—*"throwing good money away so you can hang upside down!"*

She hung up on me.

"Is everything all right?" Miss Otterbridge asked me when I came out of her office.

"A little emergency came up at home," I said, "but I told my mother I'd handle it for her."

She patted my arm. "You're a good son. And if your mother needs you, by all means go to her. You can leave now."

And miss the Yankee game?

"Oh, no, I couldn't, Miss Otterbridge. You need me to help take all those residents to the . . . *Heyyyy!"* I suddenly realized the Wartzburg was quiet. *"They didn't leave without me, did they?"*

She smiled. "Don't concern yourself, dear. These family emergencies happen. And I've arranged for several of the housekeepers to replace you and Freddy."

"Freddy? Why him?"

"Oh, I sent him home over an hour ago . . . before lunch. He's absolutely heartbroken about Slick. And now I think . . ."

I couldn't believe it! The first chance I'd ever had in my life to go to a Yankee game and I was *missing* it!

"But Miss Otterbridge! You don't understand about my family's emergency. It's over money," I said in a voice shriller than Mom's. "We're in terrible financial trouble. Debts. Bills. Even my little sister's working. And it's not going to help if I go home. The best thing I can do is . . ."

". . . stay and work?"

I nodded and she pushed her glasses up her nose, eyes welling with sympathy. "Well, if that's the case, you'll stay. And I'll see you earn some money to help out."

"Oh, thank you, Miss Otterbridge. You have no idea how much this means to me. Thank you, thank you, *thank you!*"

I could have kissed her feet till I realized she was leading me into the kitchen. "Mister Raymond," she said,
"Horace will be staying in here with you this afternoon
to clean out the pantry."

"You mean I'm not going to the game?"

Miss Otterbridge shook her head. "This will be far
more advantageous for your situation. You'll receive
double wages."

"But . . ."

"No buts, dear. This job *deserves* double. And if anyone on the board of directors questions the expense, I'll
say it was absolutely essential for kitchen hygiene and
efficiency."

She opened the wide pantry door and I stared in at
the hundreds upon hundreds of jars, cans, and bags of
food supplies. "These are already in categories," she
said, sweeping her hand past a hundred-pound sack of
wheat flour, toward a ten-foot wall of shelves. "Grains,
pasta, canned fruits, vegetables, and so on. But they've
never been arranged alphabetically. Today we'll do it."

She left me with a sponge, a pail of hot water, disin-
fectants, and a sob throbbing in my chest. How did I
end up like this? *How?* I wanted to watch Don Mattingly hit a grand-slam home run. And what was I doing? Wiping off tin lids and trying to figure out if tomatoes with basil came before plain tomato sauce.

When I was scrubbing off the bottom shelf on the
second wall, Mister Raymond poked his head in.

"Pfewww. Must be a hundred-forty in there, Ace. Don't ya want to come out and take a little breather? You been cooped up for two hours. How about some iced tea?"

"No, it's all right," I said, turning my head away from him so he wouldn't see me crying.

"You sure? The Old Timers game is over and the big one's ready to start. You could listen on my radio."

"No, no . . . I'm, uh . . . I'm fine."

"Well, it's up to you. But keep this door open, okay? You're gonna suffocate."

Little did he know I wouldn't have minded. Especially when I heard the sportscaster announce that Mattingly was up to bat. If I couldn't see him, I sure didn't want to hear about him.

To drown out the radio, I sang all the sad little Stephen Foster songs I'd learned back in grade school.

> *Gone are the days*
> *When my heart was young and gay.*
> *Gone are my friends*
> *From the . . .*

Then I started talking to myself:

" 'Tis not a pleasant thing to be a young man, alone, grief-stricken in a sweatbox on a fair July Saturday," I made up, trying to sound like a down-and-out Dickens character would in my predicament. " 'Tis a far, far more cruel and paltry world when—"

"Repeat that first line!" commanded a crisp, British voice below me.

"Sir Cecil!" The surprise of seeing him in his wheelchair in my pantry nearly sent me flying off the ladder I was using to reach a high shelf. "What're you doing here? Why aren't you at the game?"

"I loathe those vulgar, multitudinal gatherings. Now, do as I said. Only this time, pause after *alone* and *grief-stricken*. They needed more emphasis."

I stopped stacking cans of chick-peas and said the line. "Why'd you want to hear that?"

"Never mind," he said. "Where did you receive your dramatic training?"

"No place. Or, well, I was once in a movie. The director helped me. Gave me little tips now and then."

For a moment he studied me long and hard. "Young man, what would you do if someone gave you a large kettledrum? Tap it with a hairpin?"

"Oh, no, sir. I'd pound it."

"Then think of your voice as that instrument. Let it roll. Create thunder. You need discipline if you're to become a great classical actor. Use your lungs!"

"You mean holler?"

"No, not holler. *Project!* From down here," he said, patting his upper abdomen.

"Now I get it," I said. "That's what I do when I'm really mad at my sister."

"Ohhh?" His pursed lips softened and he reached in his breast pocket for a pen and used envelope. "Try this line from *Julius Caesar,*" he said as he wrote something. "Imagine you're projecting it to a roomful of sisters."

I got down from the ladder and read what he'd written. "Okay," I said. Then I looked at the last hundred cans I'd arranged, took a deep breath . . .

"Now concentrate."

. . . and pretended the cans were all Noras. *"You blocks! You stones! You worse than senseless things,"* I projected with enough force to start an earthquake.

"Better," he said as Miss Otterbridge came squealing

into the pantry followed by a wild-eyed Mister Raymond.

"What's the matter, Horace? Did you fall . . . are you injured? Or was that you, Sir Cecil?"

"The sound you heard," Sir Cecil answered, "was Mr. Hobart exercising his kettledrum. His voice is extraordinary, but he has no control over it. I'm giving him his first acting lesson."

I grabbed my sponge and scrambled back up the ladder. Man, was she going to be sore that I'd been fooling around on double wages. But no. She was listening to him describe all my acting deficiencies and how he planned to correct them before he gave me a part in a play he wanted to direct. All news to me, of course.

"What play do you have in mind?" she said. "One in this year's Dramafest?"

"Only if Mr. Hobart is committed. I should coach him an hour a day. He needs work. And I *do* mean work."

I stopped polishing a two-gallon can of peaches and looked down to see her reaction. "If Horace can accomplish for you what he does for me, you won't be disappointed," she said. "Just look at what he's done in this pantry." She was smiling up at me. "Horace, dear, come down and relax. I didn't expect you to finish half this much. You must be exhausted."

Then she took Mister Raymond's arm and pulled him, still speechless, out of the pantry. "Don't disturb them any more. Let them continue with their lesson."

Lesson? Whew! Lining up cans wasn't half as much torture as learning how to expand my diaphragm. My chest ached. I was on the verge of collapsing when Sir Cecil finally called it quits. "Till tomorrow," he said, and zipped out of the pantry in his wheelchair.

I staggered out behind him and saw Mister Raymond violently shaking his radio. "C'mon Yankees! C'mon. The bases are loaded! Let's hit a homer!"

"What's the score?" I asked.

"A seven-to-seven tie. We're in the eighth inning."

A lump welled in my throat and I found myself hurrying into Miss Otterbridge's office. "I really, really think I ought to go over to the stadium. *Now,*" I said, startling her as she worked on a pile of papers. "Crowds are brutal when a game's over. Our residents' lives will be in danger. People shove and push . . . they throw things like beer cans. Even *banana peels!*"

Her hand flew to her mouth. "Oh, my. I don't attend games. I hadn't realized. But if that's what happens, you should go help out," she said, reaching in a drawer for a ticket that she handed me along with a ten-dollar bill. "The game must be nearly over by now. Take a taxi."

She even walked me out to the gates, then sent the watchman down to the corner to whistle me a cab. While I waited for it, she relaxed a bit and asked me how my acting lesson went. "Not good," I said. "Sir Cecil thinks I'm awful."

"Awful?" she cried. "You're wrong, Horace. Over three hundred young actors and actresses have passed through these gates since Sir Cecil came to live with us and never—*not once*—has he ever taken the slightest interest in any of them. He recognizes a special talent in you. And you should be greatly honored that he wants to direct you in the Dramafest.

My cab was pulling up and she waited at the curb as the watchman got out and I got in. "Horace, I insist that you spend that hour with him every day," she called as I closed the door.

"Where to?" said the cabbie.

"Yankee Stadium and fast," I said, glancing at my watch. Maybe I'd make it for the last inning.

He took me at my word and raced his yellow Checker through the traffic at such high speed, we could've caused a sonic boom. Everything we passed was a blur till he slowed down by the stadium entrance and I saw a burned-out car, still smoking, about ten yards down the street. Obscene graffiti was spray-painted on the sidewalk near it. On the trunk was a crude outline of a cat, back arched, tail fur spiked upright.

"Second car today I've seen like that," the cabbie said as I paid him his fare. "Cat looks like he's getting electrocuted, don't he?"

"Sure does," I said, hurrying out. Wild cheering was coming from the stadium. And I was dying to get in there.

Even in a crowd of some sixty thousand sports fans, the fifteen Wartzburgers weren't hard to find. Compliments of the Actors Guild, they had field-level box seats. What caught my eye first, though, were Flora and Gayle in round straw sun hats, big as tabletops, decked with flowers. Sitting wedged in between them was my poor old buddy George. I waved when I saw him, but got no response. He just kept staring straight ahead, looking positively venomous. I knew right off I didn't want to sit near him.

Or in the box behind him, either. That's where Pearl, in a scarlet dress and enough chunky jewelry to sink a ship, was screeching, *"Yeah, Buster? Wanna know where you can stuff your Boston Red Sox?"* up at somebody in the mezzanine level.

I quickly scanned the other boxes, looking for J.D. He's always laid-back and fun to be with. I'd join him.

"Hi," I said when I found him and took the empty aisle seat on his left. "How's the game goin'?"

"How should I know?" he barked. "Think I've seen any of it with this . . . *this* . . ."He glowered down at PeeWee's head resting on his shoulder, then suddenly jumped up like he wanted to hit me. "Here! *You* take over! *You* baby-sit!"

Without a word, I exchanged places, knocking over a bunch of empty paper beer cups I hadn't noticed by PeeWee's feet. What was all the big fuss about? PeeWee looked perfectly blissful to me. Eyes closed. Mouth set in a wavy grin. Until he hiccupped and snuggled his head on my shoulder, saying, "Howyadoin' there, Jack?" I didn't think he'd even been aware of me moving in next to him.

"I'm fine," I said.

"Tha's good. Ever'thing's prosmosigus with me, too, Jack."

I stretched my neck, peering over his head to see what was happening out on the field. Man! Here I was . . . Horace Hobart in Yankee Stadium at last. Maybe I hadn't made it for the whole game, but I was there in time for the bottom half of the ninth inning. And what a thriller it was going to be, too. We were trailing the Red Sox nine to eight, Willie Randolph was on first and . . . *was it?* My heart stopped. Mattingly was going up to bat!

I nearly wept for joy watching him run out to home plate. "Come on, Don, baby!" I screamed as he wiggled his hips and steadied his bat.

The Red Sox pitcher rotated his shoulder, loosening the joints in his pitching arm, then wound up for his first throw. Man . . . I could already feel it in my bones. The ball wouldn't be any good. Neither would the sec-

ond. But the third? It was gonna head straight into Mattingly's bat and he was gonna drive it to London! This was a dream come true—being here in person, about to watch a game-winning home run and . . .

"Hey!"

PeeWee was standing in front of me, blocking my view. "Sit down!" I yelled.

"Can't, Jack. I gotsta go pee."

"Later!" I shrieked.

"Now!" he cried. "You gotsta take me to go *now!*"

I pushed him down in his seat, but he popped right back up again and started dragging me out of mine, all the while hopping around on one foot like a chicken. "What's so funny?" I snarled at J.D.

"Ya figured out yet how PeeWee got his name?" he said, doubling over with laughter.

I wanted to slug him. Especially since I'd just missed the first ball. "Stop yanking my arm!" I hollered at Pee-Wee. But he wouldn't. Not even after he'd pulled me out of our box and up the aisle steps, warning me to hurry. Halfway up, I missed the second ball.

In fact, I missed everything. Even the game-winning home run. Mattingly hit it the *exact* instant PeeWee and I stepped into the men's room, closing the door behind us. How do I know? Because I heard about fifty thousand Yankee fans going crazy.

"Be back for you in a minute," I told PeeWee, thinking I'd duck outside a sec. Maybe I could at least watch Randolph and Mattingly running.

But, of course, from where the men's room was located—kitty-corner from the main gate—I couldn't see the field. Only a mob of hot, dirty, screaming kids squeezing in on a hot-dog vendor. I gave up, swearing, and went back inside. "Okay, let's go," I yelled at Pee-

Wee. But he'd already left. Slipped right out of the men's room and disappeared. And I was responsible for him.

I tore outside again, looking left and right. "Hey, any of you seen a little old man in a pink shirt, carrying a black derby?" I called over to the kids lined up for hot dogs.

"Yeah, I seen him," said a tough-looking twelve-year-old greaser wearing a hoop earring.

"Where'd he go?"

The kid gave his buddies a sly grin and they all grinned back. "The hot-dog man slopped him with mustard 'n stuck him on a bun," he said. When his friends roared, he added, " 'N somebody ate him."

Brats! I drew myself up to my full six feet one and a half inches, leering down at them. *"You blocks! You stones! You worse than senseless things!"* I bellowed. *"Kecksies! Burs! Thou whoreson little tidy Bartholomew boar pigs!"*

They'd withered into a speechless clump and I took off. Not bad, I thought. My pantry Shakespeare was quite effective. Then I saw him. Or rather I saw a streak of hot pink, the same as in his Hawaiian shirt. "PeeWee, wait!" I called. "People're leaving . . . you'll get lost."

He'd slapped on his black derby and I could see it bobbing alongside a stream of early birds who were trying to beat it out of the stadium before the big crowds left. *"Don't you dare go out that gate!"* I screamed.

If he heard me, he wasn't paying attention. When I caught up with him, I clamped his hand in mine, feeling thoroughly justified to be dragging him behind me this time. It was obvious why he'd slipped out of my sight. Beer foam was on the corners of his mouth. He smelled

like he'd been dunked in the stuff. "How many Schlitzes did you have?" I asked.

"None, Jack."

Naturally by now there were massive stampedes rushing for the gates. People by the thousands. "You're lucky I found you. Know that?" I said as I steered him around a procession of hefty middle-aged women carrying a NEWBURGH LOVES THE YANKS banner.

His answer was a quick twist of the wrist. He was trying to slip away from me again, so I gripped him harder. "C'mon, Jack. Be good. Buy me one mo' beer," he said.

"Stop calling me Jack!" I snapped. It was getting on my nerves.

"Will if you buy me 'nother Schlitz, Jack."

The old devil. I jet-propelled him through the throngs, back to our boxes, where our cranky, red-faced group was waiting for us.

"Where the heck've you been, Ace?" George hollered when he saw me.

"Irresponsible!" roared Pearl. "Miss Otterbridge should never've allowed you to join us."

Other than the cleanup crews and a few stragglers, we were the last group to leave the stadium. I glanced back at the field, thinking what a bummer the afternoon had been. Thank heavens the Actors Guild was sending limos. A ride back to the Wartzburg in air-conditioned comfort would be the highlight of my day.

Fourteen

"It's after five, I miss our tea," Pearl said in a new and softer voice.

"They told us *right here*, now where are they?" Flora whimpered, pinching the frilly neck of her white blouse.

"I think it's because *we* are late," Gayle said.

Flora's mouth puckered. "You're probably right!"

"Aw, hell, you're both crazy!" Pearl said. "They told us to stand one block from the stadium gates and they'd be waiting from four o'clock on. They've just stranded us." She looked around at me. "Ace!" she bellowed. "You have to do something."

What could I do? George had gone to look for the limos, leaving me and J.D., the housekeepers, and Alfonso, the Cuban handyman, in charge of everybody. I peered through the thinning crowd going home and felt rotten and miserable. These darn complaints were giving me a headache.

George returned, shrugged and shook his head.

"Well, what are we going to do if our rides aren't here?" J.D. said.

"Couldn't it be that *we* are late?" Gayle repeated, and Flora beside her shook her head up and down at us.

If I heard that one more time, I was going to pop her. *Couldn't it be that we are late couldn't it be that w—*

"I told you that was stupid!" Pearl said, pushing her face at Gayle.

"Come on, forget the limos," George said. "We'll take the subway. It's quick."

"With fifteen old people?" J.D. muttered.

"My feets is shot, man, somebody gonna have to carry me," PeeWee said, tugging my arm and blowing his beery breath in my face. "Just do the fastest thing. We's tired." From the looks of the group, he was dead right.

"I don't like the subway system," Flora said. She stamped her foot. "I never did before, and I don't ride them now. The nice people get mugged on them."

"You're safe with us," George promised, extending his arm to her like some knight in a movie. She looked into his face, tilted her head to see if he could possibly be telling her the truth, and finally took his arm. He led off with her and the rest of us followed them, walking slowly to the station. I felt relieved when it was only a block away, because both Pearl and PeeWee were hanging on me. I had to drag them every step. All the time I was praying that we wouldn't get spotted by the Piranhas and have our cover blown for good!

Miss Otterbridge had given Alfonso emergency money, so when we got to the booth, he bought the tokens. The platform was jammed. There were baseball fans, transit cops, and hoods everywhere, but none I recognized.

What a relief when the train came! We all took George's advice to squeeze in with the smaller crowd that was shoving into the last car. We'd never have made it in the middle ones. I had a good grip on Pearl and PeeWee, but still we were the last ones on, barely getting in before the doors slid shut.

"Nobody's going to offer us seats," Flora whined. "On the subway people are animals!" She closed her eyes and clung, white-knuckled, to the same center pole

most of the rest of us were holding on to. Alfonso, behind me, had a little group he was taking care of near
the back door.

"Tell Flora to be quiet, somebody will hear her,"
Jacqueline whispered to me.

"I don't care if they do!" Flora said even louder.

I cringed and looked over the heads of the old folks
into the crowd, and caught the droopy-eyed stare of a
tall girl close enough to me to spit straight in my eyes.
She had a Mohawk haircut, green eye-goop, blackheads
on her nose, shark's teeth for earrings, and an electrocuted cat tattooed on her shoulder. Her front was like
torpedoes and the halter she was wearing didn't hide
much.

Blink, I thought, why don't you blink? But her
hooded spook eyes stared straight at me and then at
George and J.D. The guys were so busy with our
charges that they didn't see her. Her lip curled and
suddenly I wondered if she recognized us from somewhere. Where?

I shrank into my shoes, trying to disappear, then
shifted behind Pearl's beefy bulk. Finally I had to look
down. I tried concentrating on the top of PeeWee's
derby. I wasn't going to look up again until the train
stopped at the next station and the big pig got off.
Suppose she didn't? Suppose she had more punk
friends on the train? Suppose they stayed on until we
got off and they followed us to the Wartzburg?

"What's the matter with the train?" Pearl said, looking up at me. "It's not going fast enough."

"It seems slow to me, too," I said.

Then she noticed the looming face of the punk
rocker. Pearl's head snapped back and she yelled, "You
look like one of those pyromaniacs I've heard about!

Get away from us or I'm going to report you to the transit police."

That dumb Pearl. The Mohawk-headed girl was furious. "Shut up, you old witch, or I'll give you something hot right now."

The crowd pressing around us shrank back. Flora squealed. I took a step and came down on PeeWee's heel. He cried out in pain. J.D. and George saw the punk rocker; their mouths dropped open. Jacqueline and Leslie gasped.

"What's going on?" Jacqueline said.

"Nothin', nothin'," I whispered, realizing the stupid train was going slower by the second.

"Sumthin' smells bad, Jack," PeeWee said. "Like burning rubber."

"Yeah!" J.D. said, sniffing.

The punk rocker, glaring at all of us now, grinned. Whatever the smell was, it began to fog up the air. Pearl coughed and couldn't stop. A weirdo in goggles said, "Whaddya think is happenin'?"

Nobody answered him. The train squeaked along the tracks. Lights flickered. And then, with a lurch, we pulled into the station.

The doors opened. The crowd poured out. New passengers came on. The sharp smell hung in the air. The punk rocker wasn't getting off! Still staring, she said, "Are *you* going to call me a pyromaniac?"

"No, no!" I said real fast.

"Are you?" she said to J.D. and George.

"What're you tryin' to pull?" J.D. snapped back, real tough.

"You Mohawk-headed harlot, you trash, you pyromaniac arsonist! Get off this car! I'm going to report you so you can be arrested and disemboweled," Pearl said.

The three of us Falcons looked at each other and moved in on Pearl Bigmouth, blocking her completely. "Get outta my way, boys!" she bleated, pounding on my back.

Outside, a whistle blew. The punk rocker heard it and, just before the doors began to close, leapt off the train. "Take this, you old bat!" she yelled, and tossed in a firecracker that hit the floor and went off as the train left the station.

Boomooooooom! it went, knocking us back against the walls. Smoke filled the air. Jacqueline and Linda screamed. George ran to the emergency cord and yanked it almost out of the socket. I heard the old folks whimper like kittens. Then they stood absolutely still and silent, except for Gayle. She cursed Pearl for causing the trouble, and one of the other passengers, too, began to accuse her.

Suddenly the train jerked to a halt, sending Flora and Gayle flying up the aisle like kids on roller skates. J.D. caught them and made them sit down on the side. The lights flashed, went off, flashed on again, and then went off for good. We were in pitch darkness, our mouths and lungs full of thick, acid-tasting smoke. But at least there wasn't any fire we could see. Everybody on the train was coughing now. I felt Pearl lunge into me and slide to the floor before I could catch her. I bent down next to her. "Hey, are you okay?"

But she didn't answer.

I passed my hand over her face in the dark. "Everybody! Pearl's out cold, her eyes are shut, I can feel 'em with my hand."

"Quiet!" a stranger's voice yelled. "They're announcing something."

The P.A. system made a scratchy sound. Sputtered.

Then a voice, a man's voice, said, *"Polgeze dlay strumpen wrong polderholz kerplumming."*

Flora was crying. "Be quiet! We can't hear the announcement!" a passenger shouted. "Shhh! Here it is again."

"Polgeze berpdelay schrump wrong ploderhltzee kermuming!"

"What dee hell ees it saying?" Alfonso the handyman yelled.

"The conductor's just said the train's broken down and somebody's coming," another passenger screamed. "Can't you understand English!"

"Shut up!" George yelled, now kneeling next to me near Pearl. "One of these old people has passed out. Maybe she's dying!"

"Aw, don't worry about it," Gayle said, sounding as calm and cool as a cucumber. "Pearl always does that to get attention. When help comes, she snaps right to."

"Oh, yeah! Well, *I* think she's unconscious!" I shouted back at Gayle. I was so sick of her, I hoped Pearl *was* unconscious.

"I tole you we was tired," PeeWee said, shuffling his feet near me. "So dark in here, likely she thinks she be sleepin' in her bed now."

Fifteen

Pearl was out cold. She had to be carried out of the train on a stretcher. The conductor had rescued the other passengers with a flashlight, explaining before he led them out that somebody had monkeyed with the undercarriage of the train while it was laid up outside Yankee Stadium. The third rail had ignited the engine and along with the firecracker had caused a lot of smoke.

Following the conductor, J.D., Alfonso, and the housekeepers escorted the Wartzburg residents, who were pretty shook up by then, along the bench wall in the subway tunnel all the way to the station platform.

Not long after they left, George and I were following the stretcher-bearers, big muscle-bound guys who moved like pro halfbacks. The tunnel was all lit up with lights that cops had brought in. I'd just peered up, over, and around one of the guys' shoulders at Pearl's face—milk custard with a smear of plum lipstick—and caught a twitch.

"Her eyelids fluttered, I saw it!" George said.

"Yeah, me too. Is she coming to?" I yelled at the guy. No answer.

George barked, "Speak to *her*, that's what's supposed to help."

Well, right there with all those transit workers and firemen around, I wasn't going to do it. I was afraid she might talk back. A cop on the platform noticed the stretcher and raised a bullhorn to his mouth. "Injured!

Move back, make way! Hey, stupid," he said to us as we
tried to catch up, "outta the way!"

We ignored him and rushed through the gate and up
the stairs behind Pearl. The hot air hit me at the top and
I sucked it into my smoked-out lungs. Whew! It was
good to be out of there.

George knocked me in the ribs. "Look at that!" He
pointed to a huge van marked NEW YORK FIRE DEPART-
MENT ANTI-ARSON TEAM.

A bunch of uniformed guys with red caps were coming out of it onto the street. They swarmed through the
traffic and the bystanders, stopping some to ask questions or going straight down the stairs of the subway
station past us. They looked angry. George watched
them intently; I think he wanted to tell them something.

Six other emergency vehicles were half parked on
the sidewalk at crazy angles. Pearl's attendants had
headed for a yellow, blue, and white ambulance. The
late afternoon light made all the colors gleam. The
white looked kind of pink.

"Ya see 'em?" George said, looking for our group.

"Yes, hope they went on back to the Wartzburg."

Pearl's chrome stretcher wheels made contact with
the pavement.

"Move it on over there," the ambulance attendant
yelled, pointing to the next ambulance. "For that pa-
tient, ya need a Greyhound, ha-ha-ha!"

"You're real funny, man!" one of our big guys said.
"We're bringin' her here. Get somebody to check her
out."

One of the arson officers joined our group. "She got
some ID?"

"Hey, Pearly, they want to talk to you," George said

in that wheedly little voice people use on babies or pets.
I'd never heard George do that. She didn't answer him.

Pressed under arms that were folded over her chest
was her pocketbook. As soon as the officer touched her
fingers to pull her hands away so he could see, life
flooded into her gray face. "Muggers!" she yelled, keeping her eyes tightly shut.

"It's okay, Pearl!" I said, and patted her shoulder
twice.

"Yeah, Pearl," murmured George. "It's all right, the
nurse here wants to check you out, okay?"

"My chest hurts like hell!" she whined. "I can't
breathe." We heard her wheeze and I thought how mad
Miss Otterbridge was going to be about our taking the
old folks on the subway.

"Think she's having a heart attack?" George whispered. "Pearl? Can you open your eyes?"

"She doesn't want to let go of her purse, sir," I told
the officer. But then the small black-haired CPR nurse
who was with the ambulance came over and firmly took
the pocketbook away and applied the stethoscope to
her chest. Then right away they put Pearl on oxygen.

"It's not a heart attack, fellas, relax! It's anoxia," the
nurse said. "My name's Kurtz. She your mom or
grandmom or what?"

"No relationship to me!" George said.

"Me either!"

"Oh, a friend," the woman said. "We want to take her
to Bronx Lebano—"

"I'm not going to the hospital, not on your life! Tell
her, Ace. Take me back to the Wartzburg, I know my
rights!" Pearl screamed.

The nurse was trying to keep her hooked to the life-
support stuff. So they put Pearl inside the ambulance

and we climbed inside with her. The driver started the motor. Miss Kurtz was monitoring Pearl. The ambulance went straight toward the Wartzburg, driving through the gates and up to the delivery entrance like we were an order of meat.

"Here we are," the driver sang out cheerfully. He jumped out and went around to open the back doors. "Time to get you out, Miss Orient."

When the doors opened, I saw Miss Otterbridge standing on the steps. My heart sank. She was going to fire us, I was sure. I leaned down and wiped Pearl's sweaty forehead with a wrinkled Kleenex from my pocket.

"We're home, Pearl, you're going to feel a lot better soon, I promise," George said.

Pearl sighed.

Miss Otterbridge shouted to the driver, "Our orderlies will bring her in, young man." Then, "Ace! George! Are you all right?"

She wanted to know about *us?*

"We're okay, but, uh . . . Pearl's got chest pains."

The medical team wheeled Pearl in her bed out of the ambulance onto the lawn, and the Wartzburg orderlies in their white suits came and got her.

"Put her in her room!" Miss Otterbridge called to them.

They took her inside the building. Miss Otterbridge had sounded irked and I wondered if she thought Pearl was faking too.

"Hey," I whispered. "She really is sick, Miss Otterbridge. She almost died."

George nodded. "The paramedic said she has angina."

Suddenly Miss Otterbridge's face softened and she

looked sympathetic. She thanked the driver and the nurse for their care, signed a paper, and turned to go back inside with us.

"Did the rest of the gang . . . I mean, the others . . . make it?" George said. We were walking around to the front of the house together.

"Oh, yes, all of them did. They're fine, just fine! J.D. went home already. I was so worried when you two wonderful boys were late. It was an agony of waiting."

"Aww . . ." said George. "You didn't have to worry about *us.*"

Her eyes narrowed. "You know, I'm going to sue that limousine company. Just wait! So's the Actors Guild, of course. No excuse for such negligence. Well, everybody's in the dining room. They wanted cocoa to quiet their nerves. Plenty for you . . ."

"Cocoa?" George said with a hot, shiny face.

"Oh, no, thanks! We just want to get home, Miss Otterbridge," I said.

"You know, Ace, I don't know how to thank you for thinking of going to that game and realizing how much you might be needed. It's amazing for someone so young to be that thoughtful! I admire your selfless kindness so much . . . you don't mind if I . . ." Miss Otterbridge leaned toward me. I didn't feel it was right to back off the way I did when I was just a kid.

She kissed me. It wasn't too bad; she smelled like the lilac perfume Mom wears on Sundays.

"It really wasn't anything," I told her, embarrassed. Even if she didn't, I knew why I'd really gone to the game.

"And you, George. I know you didn't want to work at the Wartzburg in the beginning. But you are intelli-

gent, so responsible, and amazingly good at the care of the elderly."

"I am?"

"I think you should consider it as a career in case . . . in case things in the theater don't work out for you as they quite often . . ."

"Oh, hey! I'm not thinkin' so much about that anymore . . ." George said, flushing purple.

"You remember what I told you, then," she said with a smile.

"Well . . . okay . . . I will. . . ."

"I must be getting in to look after Pearl now, but I think you both were wonderful." She turned and went inside.

For a minute George and I stood there without saying a word. Then we looked at each other, grinned, and started home. We were just too dazed by all that had happened to change into bag-lady clothes.

Sixteen

I stood in front of the door to The Pits, shopping bags in one hand, key in the other. I'd just narrowly escaped being fried in a subway fire and now I had to face a grilling by the folks. How much trauma could a poor guy take in one day?

Without Superman's X-ray vision, I knew what everybody inside was doing. Dad was in his Barcalounger, either snoozing or watching a Saturday-night special. Nora was on the floor, counting her dog money, ready to pounce on me for what I owed her, plus interest. And Mom? Easy. Mom was sitting at the kitchen table in her pink robe, poring over a stack of bills. In one minute she'd have Dad out of his Barcalounger so they could kill me for ordering the Gravity Guide System.

I stuck the key in the lock, then pulled it out again. It was only nine. Maybe I wouldn't go in just yet. Maybe I'd sit on the stairs a couple of hours.

As I tiptoed away from the door I heard a faint click, then noticed a sliver of light shine out from the peephole. Somebody had lifted the cover. An eye—a big, round, snoopy green eye—was peering out into the hall, watching me.

"Hey, Mom . . . Dad!" Nora hollered as she swung the door open. "Horace is home and he's not burned up, or anything! Ewww, sick, Horace . . . whatcha got in all those dirty bags?"

"Mind your own business," I said, following her inside with my Salvation Army clothes.

Mom flew out of the living room with her hair full of plastic curlers. "Ohh, Horace, honey. We've been so scared," she said, throwing her arms around me. "Are you all right?"

Now Dad was squeezing in between us to pat my shoulder. "You okay, son?"

Hey? What'd come over them?

"We all saw you on the news . . ." Nora said as she wrestled my bags away from me. "Boy, you should've seen your face, Horace . . . gagging and coughing. Mom cried when she saw you. Then we saw ambulances and stretchers and cops and fire engines and all those old actors you were rescuing and George and J.D. Was anybody killed?"

"News? About the fire?" I said, confused. "You mean it was on TV?"

Mom was glancing into the living room as if somebody was in there.

Now Dad was doing it.

"We were playing Monopoly and wouldn't have known anything," Nora was blabbing on, "if Raven hadn't called us. She's the one who saw the news first."

"Raven?" I said. *"She called?"* Then I saw her— Raven Galvez, the goddess of J. F. Kennedy High, sitting on the couch in the living room.

"Hi, Ace," she said a little shyly, like she wasn't sure if I'd be happy to see her.

My stomach rose and fell and my heart started galloping like a runaway horse. She'd never looked more beautiful! All dressed in white; her velvet skin a deep, coppery summer tan; black silk hair floating over the sleeves of her ruffled organdy blouse. I just stared at her, mouth open.

How had I survived for so long without seeing her?

"*Nincompoop!* Don't just stand there . . . say something to her!" barked Nora. "She's been here waiting for you. She even called Miss Whoosey Doo at the Wartzburg to see if you got hurt!"

"Whatsa matter, son? You inhale a lot of smoke?" Dad asked.

I eyed Raven and forced myself to cough. "I guess . . . maybe. A little. I don't remember," I said as I lowered myself onto the couch.

Mom smiled apologetically at Raven. "I'm afraid Ho.ace is still in a state of shock after the ordeal he's been through." Then she turned to me, smiling. "Can I get you something to drink, honey? Something cold?"

I nodded.

"Coke? Lemonade? Iced tea?"

I nodded again.

"Which, Horace?"

"Coke," Nora said for me.

The Monopoly set was pushed to one end of the coffee table and four half-filled glasses of soda were sitting on a tray in the center, next to a bowl of popcorn. Nora crowded her way onto the couch between Raven and me, finished what was in one of the glasses, then tapped the bottom so all the ice cubes tumbled into her mouth.

"Horace, wanna hear something interesting?" she said with her cheeks pouched like a hamster's. "Raven's not reading to that blind man anymore. The old phony was faking it . . . his dark glasses and cane were a big put-on."

I felt my power of speech coming back to me. "*Ohhh?*" I said to Raven.

She nodded. "It's true, Ace. He's a fake. I saw him parking a car—a brand-new, bright tomato-red Alfa Romeo—in front of his building yesterday."

Thrilled as I was to see her, it broke my heart to find her so hurt and disillusioned. If only I could reach over and pull her close to me, I thought. Wrap my arms around her.

Only I couldn't, of course. Not with Nora between us. Or the folks still up.

"If you ask me," Dad said as he settled back into his Barcalounger, "that old lecher ought to be locked up!"

"Don't get carried away, Barney," Mom said as she came back from the kitchen and handed me my Coke. I thanked her, but I would've been a lot more grateful if she'd done something with her curlers.

"Raven did the right thing," she said.

"Oh, what?" I asked.

"Lemme tell him . . ." shrieked Nora.

"Not with your mouth full!"

Nora spit the ice cubes back into her glass and said, "She walked over to his car and told him off. But what she should've done was wait till he got out of his car, then she should've kicked him. Right where it hurts!"

"Nora!" cried Mom.

"Well, she should have!"

I felt my face burn from the neck on up. What was this? A conspiracy to drive Raven away? "Raven . . . look. I'm really sorry about all this," I said.

"Oh, don't be, Ace."

"You have no idea how sorry . . ." My voice was breaking.

She started laughing. "Aw, come on, Ace . . . don't be silly. It's not the end of the world. I'll get another job."

"Job?"

"Sure. As a waitress, maybe. And anyway, that's not the most important thing to me right now. What is,

though," she said, cutting her eyes at me the way she did back in the good old days, "is that nothing happened to you in that fire tonight."

That eye business nearly did me in. I rubbed my hands up and down over my kneecaps, itching to be alone with her. Her hair. Her eyes. Her lips. Her skin. I was going wild!

"What's the matter with your knees?" said Nora.

"Nothing!" I snapped.

Wasn't anybody ever going to bed?

Mom was bringing out more popcorn!

"Raven, why don't you tell Horace what Miss Otterbridge told you when you called her?" she said as she refilled the bowl on the table.

"Oh, yes, I will," said Raven. "Thanks for reminding me. . . ." I was looking over Nora's head at her feathery, jet-black eyelashes. "Well, she just couldn't have been nicer, Ace."

"Who?"

"Miss Otterbridge. When I called her. She said you were loyal and responsible, one of her best employees ever . . ." Lord! She was cutting her eyes at me again. ". . . and you'll love this, Ace. She said you were magnificently heroic."

Nora snickered and Dad sighed from his Barcalounger as if this conversation was getting too much for him. But Raven, she was giving me one of those dimpled smiles that totally wipes me out.

"Okay, it's time! Time for Raven to go home now," I said, springing off the couch like I'd been sitting on a hot plate.

For some reason, Mom seemed to think that meant I wanted to get rid of Raven. "But Horace, you just got

here. And I'm sure she'd love to hear about the subway fire."

I grabbed Raven's hand. "Don't worry, Ma. I'll tell her all about it while I'm walking her home."

As soon as we were safely out of viewing range from the peephole, I reached for her, fully intending to give her a kiss so passionate, she'd be in danger of fainting. "Raven," I whispered, working my way up to it, "it's really good to see you. . . ."

"Who's up there?" screamed a voice from the landing below us. *"I hear you! And if you're somebody who doesn't belong in this building, I'll blow my police whistle!"*

I gripped Raven's hand tighter and swallowed. "It is I," I said in my foghorn, in my best English. "Horace Nelson Hobart. I live in apartment five-J."

"Who's with you?"

"A friend who reads to the blind."

There were a few shuffling footsteps, then a moment later I looked down at the bottom of the stairs and saw Mrs. Swann, the little chinless lady from 4-G who was the president of the Neighborhood Crime Watch Association. She was peeking up at us over the handrail. "Oh, it *is* you . . . the boy who was in that horror movie," she said, clutching a bag of garbage. "Well, you can't be too careful these days . . . you never know who's lurking in the hallways."

Forget it. There was no use trying to kiss Raven again until we were out on the street where there was a dark, secluded doorway I could duck her into. I knew just the one, too. Perfect. The entrance to a defunct bookstore a block away, halfway between my building and hers.

I was in a hurry to get there, but Raven, who didn't know the surprise I was planning, wasn't. "Hey, Ace

. . . slow down, would you?" she said when we got
outside. "You're not rescuing *me* from a fire, okay?"

I altered my running walk. "How's this?"

She laughed. "Oh, you nut, you wonderful, heroic
nut! I've really missed you, y'know that?"

I caught my reflection in the window of Vinnie's Deli
and stood up straighter. "I missed you, too," I said.
"And I kept calling, but you were never home. What
were you reading to that old blind phony, anyway? The
Encyclopedia Britannica?"

Her face grew long, then, just as we got in front of
Grimbacher's Dry Cleaners on the corner, she suddenly stopped. "Ace, there's something I've got to tell
you. Kevin isn't old."

"Who's Kevin?"

"Ay, caramba!" She rolled her eyes. "The guy I was
reading to."

"What is he? Middle-aged?"

"Twenty-five."

"Twenty-five? Hey, you weren't involved with him,
were you? Other than reading, I mean."

"I was, but I won't be! Ever again!" she spit out, dark
eyes igniting. "All last week I'd been considering telling
him *sayonara.* Even *before* I saw him parking that red
Alfa Romeo of his!"

"Why? Because you sensed he wasn't blind?"

She shook her head. "No, he had me snowed on that,
the rat! It's just, well, that he got too possessive and he
. . . oh, I don't want to talk about it! Let's just put it this
way, Ace. You're a hero and he's a *zorrillo!* That's Span-
ish for *skunk.*"

So he'd been possessive of *my* girl, had he? And she'd
really fallen for him, for a while, anyway. Probably
hadn't thought about me in weeks.

I was so down in the mouth thinking about it, I walked along, not talking, not noticing other people on the street, or even where we were, till I realized we were passing a Chock Full O' Nuts coffee shop. Then it hit me. We'd already gone by it—the entrance to the bookstore.

How was I going to show Raven I was a great lover now? Forget it, I wasn't. Not unless she invited me up to her apartment. *Would she?*

Crossing the street to get to her block, she squeezed my arm. "Aw, come on, Ace . . . let's cheer up. It's great being together again. Tell me a story—the first funny story that pops into your head."

At that moment, all the circuits in my head were on hold. I could think of nothing, funny or otherwise. Except that we were about to be run over by a big Schlitz beer delivery truck rumbling around the corner.

I grabbed Raven and did a flying leap onto the curb with her. She didn't appear the least bit fazed; she was still waiting for a story. "Thought of one yet?" she asked.

Yeah, I had. Only not funny. The word *Schlitz* made me think of my miserable time at the game with Pee-Wee. I told Raven every sordid detail, and for some odd reason she thought it was an absolute riot. Hilarious. After she'd wiped her eyes and stopped laughing, I said, "Okay, Raven . . . now it's your turn. You tell me a funny story."

She flicked a wave of black silk hair off her cheek. "Hmm . . . let's see. I can never think of anything funny the way you can, Ace. But I'll tell you something cute. Freddy called. Know what he did today?"

"I thought he stayed with Slick."

"Oh, yeah . . . he did. He stayed by his bed, playing

nursemaid for hours. But the cute part was, he fixed him a pot of *homemade chicken soup!* Then, because Slick was too sore to sit up and eat it, you know what your great Falcon leader did?"

"What? Ate it himself?"

"No. Spoon-fed every drop of it to Slick."

Now *that* just killed me! The one day Freddy's had off from the Wartzburg in weeks—and what did he do? Ended up serving food and feeding somebody anyway. I couldn't stop laughing.

"Oh, come on . . . it's not that funny," said Raven.

"But it is, it is."

An elderly couple passing by us with a shaggy yellow Pekinese stared at me like I was certifiable. Still I couldn't stop.

Then I saw Raven take a key out of the little white macramé bag she was carrying. The key sobered me up fast. We were in front of her building and I started panicking. Was this to be the setting for our night's farewell? Under the harsh light of her entrance, on the sidewalk, in public?

I held my breath. She had to invite me up, I'd die if she didn't.

"Want to come up, Ace?"

I blew out my breath. "Yeah, I guess. You're sure it's okay?"

"Sure I'm sure it's okay."

I followed her inside, remembering the first time she'd invited me up to her apartment. I'd been so nervous, I told her I couldn't because my mother needed me.

Well, tonight . . . whoopee . . . I was going to make up for it. It was two flights up and SHAZAM!

As we reached the second-floor landing, Raven

turned to me, grinning. "Bet I know what you're thinking."

"Ha-ha . . . you do?"

"That some lunatic's gonna jump out with a police whistle."

"Oh, yeah, ha-ha. Right."

Oh boy! The lights were out in the living room when she turned the lock and pushed the door open. *Think,* I commanded myself. *Think of something romantic to say to her!* But what? That her eyes were like Hershey Kisses? No, she'd think it was corny. *Think! Think!* What would Nevada Culhane, my cowboy detective— the world's greatest lover—say to his favorite woman? Probably something nice about her body.

"Umm, Raven," I whispered, "you know you have the curviest . . ."

"*Quién es? Eres tú, Raven?*" called her mother.

"*Sí, Mamá. Ace está conmigo.*"

"*Ohh, Dios mío! Está bien?*"

"*Sí, Mamá.*"

Okay, Mrs. Galvez, now that you know Raven's home and I'm fine, go back to sleep, I was thinking. But Mrs. Galvez hadn't been in bed. She'd been in the bathroom, applying cold cream. She came into the living room and flicked on a ceiling light so bright, we all could have performed heart surgery under it.

"Horacito!" she cried. "Joo haff no idee how whorried I haff been seence I saw dee news about dee sobeway fire. I pray and pray that joo no get hort. I no can go to bed."

"That's *muy* nice of you. *Gracias, muchas gracias,*" I said. "But I didn't get one teeny, *pequeña* scratch. See? So now, ha-ha, you can go right to bed. Ha-ha. To sleep."

She wiped her face with a tissue, all the while jabbering something quickly to Raven about *gelado,* Coca-Cola, and Doritos, then she hollered, *"Papá! Papá! Levántate ahora,"* down the hallway, *"Horacito está aquí! Nada le pasó. Carlos! Sylvia! Levántate! Levántate!"*

"What's going on?" I said to Raven.

"She's getting everybody up . . . the whole family. She wants to celebrate."

Seventeen

By Monday afternoon, less than forty-eight hours after the subway fire, the cops had locked up two arson suspects: Josie the Hot Wire and Elvira the Torch.

It took tear gas and half the force of the Bronx 50th Police Precinct to ferret them out of the condemned building where they were holed up. Both punks came out fighting like savages. Their capture got incredible news coverage. Even the *Times*—the paper that never goes in for sensationalism—carried a front page picture of Josie biting her arresting officer.

"Something's funny. Look at these close-ups!" George said the next night when he, J.D., and I were inside the employees' men's room we'd come across on an off-limits corridor at Grand Central. It was just a hole in the wall with dirt-caked tiles, one doorless stall, and a collection of buckets and rancid string mops, but nobody was ever in there so we'd been using the place to change out of our bag-lady gear. George spread the centerfold of the *Daily News* open on the floor and peeled off his scarf and rain slicker.

J.D. was slipping into a clean blue T-shirt. "I'm looking at them. What's the deal? Neither of those girls has a Mohawk like the girl we saw on the train."

"Think it's case of mistaken identity?" I said, tightening my sneaker laces.

George, dressed now, moved toward the door. "There's only one explanation. The punk girls aren't just a gang acting on their own. They're part of an

organization . . . an *arson* organization. Arson's big business in the Bronx."

"Wait a minute! I don't get it," J.D. said, blocking his way. "You think a whole organization set the train on fire?"

"Nope, but I think everything's connected . . ." George walked around J.D., heading through the night crowd toward the subway station. We had to catch up to hear what he was saying. "The punks make themselves too obvious. Their clothes are wild. They're always playing with fire, always begging for attention. Real criminals don't do that. They use subterfuge . . . purposely plan things to throw the cops off."

Finally I caught up with him in a space wide enough for the three of us to walk together. "So what does it all mean?" I said.

"That the punks are a smoke screen. They cover for the *real* arsonists. Remember what happened the night Flame and Ember and their crowd chased us to the Bronx Model Youth League center?"

"Yeah, they burned Ace's rump," J.D. said, heh-heh-ing.

"More than that. They were raising so much fuss on the streets while they were doing it that the cops were out chasing *them* when the big building across from the Wartzburg went up in flames."

"What I still don't get," J.D. said, dodging a guy with his hand out at the top of the stairs leading down to our train, "is how the big business part fits in."

George sighed. "People are making money! Crooked landlords collect fire insurance. Arsonists get paid for setting fires. The punk girls get paid for being a smoke screen."

"Who's paying them?"

"A mastermind. The person or persons directing the crimes."

"Ah-hah!" I said, catching his drift. "Probably the *Piranhas!*" I thought I'd figured out where George's analytical mind was leading him, but he was shaking his head.

"No, no. Somebody much tougher. A strategist. Somebody who knows just when and where to strike. A clever, powerful, conniving, twisted . . ."

I sucked in my breath. *"Ein Fuehrer?"*

"Definitely."

Someone who'd come to the same conclusion as George was Pearl. The two of them were hooked like addicts on the subject of arson. After dinner every night they watched the news together, discussing their arson theories. His was based on logic; hers on rumors. Most of them had come from her friend Louie the fryman at La Bombola China Grande.

She'd told me about Louie the day of the fire drill, but I hadn't paid much attention. By now she was fully recovered from her "near death" the night of the Yankee game. Her convalescence, however, had nearly killed off the staff.

For days she lay on a chaise in the sun-room, milking the tale of her collapse. She told everyone, especially timid Belva Bithell, how her spirit left her body that fateful night, floated out of the ambulance, and rose to heaven through a dark shaft. At the end of the shaft, she was greeted by a celestial band playing "Some Enchanted Evening." Ezio Pinza, the late star of the old musical *South Pacific*, was singing to her.

"Come with me, Pearl, darling!" he'd said to her, she

claimed. "Come with me to Parrr-a-dise." Every time
she told it, her eyelids fluttered.

Much to the regret of everybody at the Wartzburg,
she'd turned down Mr. Pinza's offer.

"Tell me about it again, Pearl!" Slick would beg. He
was the only person at the Wartzburg who never tired
of the story. "Same thing happened to me once when I
was unconscious," he confided to her. "Only there
wasn't nobody singin' to me, or nothin'. Just stars. Then
this feeling like you had, of being in a dark shaft."

He was careful not to mention that Freddy had beat
him up. In front of Miss Otterbridge he kept up the
pretense of having been smashed by a truck. And she
took a real motherly interest in him. Every day she'd
inspect his bruises and warn him not to exert himself.
Of course, he didn't.

Life as Falcons seemed close to normal now that he
was back with us. But George, J.D., and I did notice one
thing. On or off the job, Slick and Freddy were insepa-
rable. They'd made a sort of peace with each other the
day Freddy'd sat by Slick's bedside.

What amazed me was that after Freddy'd beat the
beans out of him, Slick wasn't holding a grudge!

"Man, how could I get sore at him?" he asked me.
"Freddy done what he done out of concern. I'm his
buddy, y'see, and he's real sensitive. Thinking I'd end
up a no-good disco bum was making him sick."

To keep Freddy from worrying, Slick gave up discos
and bun-hugging pants forever. And Freddy had come
to an important understanding of Slick. Slick needed to
dance, he realized. To do classical dance. His entrechats
and tour jetés were his ticket to the future.

"Why didn't I figure it out sooner?" Freddy said to
me one day in the kitchen. "Ya see, Ace, Slick's ballerina

stuff is the same to him as airplanes is to me . . . it's what's gonna get him somewheres. I mean, we all know he ain't got too many smarts, right? So he's gotta do what he does best. And if that's flappin' his arms and pointin' his toes, I gotta make sure he keeps doing it."

Freddy kept his word. With Raven's help, he researched ballet schools in New York, decided the Dumont Health Club wasn't good enough, and made Slick sign up for classes at the American Ballet Company every weekday after he finished work.

Every now and then he'd sit in on one of Slick's classes and the next day we got a report of his progress. He'd say something like "Slick's *elevation* is getting better." Or "He done some real classy cabrioles yesterday." Then George, J.D., or I would say, "What's that?" and he'd say, "Dopes! It's how he leaps off the floor! Or "That means scissor-kicking while he's up in the air."

Meanwhile, Raven had found herself a new job. Or rather my mom had found it for her. She was working full time for Mr. Papadopoulos in Gristede's meat department and she and Mom took lunchbreaks together.

Sometimes up at the Wartzburg, scrubbing pots, I'd fantasize one of their conversations:

"Like to try a piece of my mango, Mrs. Hobart?"

"Sure, thanks, Raven. By the way, did you know that Horace has a new zit behind his ear? He was picking it yesterday."

"Oh, ha-ha, really, Mrs. Hobart? Bet he gets them because he's so horny."

"You don't mean he gets fresh with you, Raven?"

"Yeah, sure. All the time. He's always trying to duck me into dark doorways."

"How disgusting! Raven, you make sure you're never alone with him."

Just when I developed their conversation to the point
where Mom was telling Raven I had athlete's foot and
used to sleep with a rag doll named Happykins, I'd feel
Mister Raymond tapping me.

"Hey, Ace . . . that pot's clean enough. You'll scrub
a hole through it."

By August first I was sick of the bag-lady paraphernalia. I knew if I had to ride the subway once more in my
itchy, smelly horse blanket, I'd rot. Why were we still
wearing disguises anyway? We hadn't seen a Piranha in
weeks. And there wasn't a sign of a punk rocker stalking
us either.

In my opinion, George and his co-detective, Pearl,
were off the wall with their organized-arson theory.

"Well, this is it!" I said to him and J.D. as we rode
home on the IRT train one night. "After tomorrow I'm
wearing regular clothes. I'm meeting Raven after work
Friday night and I can't do it smelling like a dead
horse."

George shrugged. "Okay . . . then you're not coming up to the Bronx with me anymore. That punk
rocker on the train saw *us* just as clear as we saw her. It's
been quite a while. The gang is lying low, letting the
two that were caught take the rap. When the mastermind is ready, they'll strike again."

"Swell!" I said, feeling mad. "I'll wear the stuff and
reek, then. That'll give Raven another excuse for not
kissing me."

"What!" J.D. said, widening his eyes. "As soon as she
gets a load of that big, booming voice that Sir Cecil's
been developing in your chest, she'll fall on her knees."

That night I couldn't get Raven out of my mind. I kept thinking of her and her silky black hair, her Hershey Kisses eyes, and her curvy body. I could hardly even talk to her much this summer. I wanted her to know about the danger the Falcons and I faced every day going up to the Bronx, and about Sir Cecil working me so hard . . .

Mom, Dad, Nora, and I were in the living room watching an ancient flick on TV. But I couldn't concentrate, thinking of Raven.

"You seem extra quiet tonight, Horace . . ." Mom said, jolting me out of my reverie. "Anything wrong?"

I pretended to be really into the movie we were seeing. "Boy, Hollywood doesn't make 'em this way anymore. Cowboys, Indians, massacres!"

"Corny and stupid and dumb, you mean," Nora said.

Dad, in his Barcalounger, started to snore and Nora's shrill voice drowned out the TV movie. "Mom, can you bee-lieve this old black-and-white junk? Just look at the guys who are Apaches; they're not real Indians, they're all Puerto Ricans!"

I sat on the couch, staring at the screen. The band of Puerto Rican Apaches, plastered with warpaint and feathers, had circled an overturned stagecoach. Arrows and bullets zinged in every direction. Everybody was dead or dying and the U.S. Cavalry coming to the rescue was only a cloud of dust on the horizon. Mom was ignoring Nora, who was still moaning, and I was concentrating on the stagecoach driver—a guy with a bruised and battered hat who was firing off two pistols at once. He was terrific!

Funny . . . in a way, he looked familiar. . . .

"If we had cable, we wouldn't have to watch this old

junk. We could see new movies and MTV!" Nora
whined.

I got off the couch and crawled toward the set, squint-
ing so I could focus better on the driver.

Zap!

An arrow whizzed through his hat, flew it right off his
head. *That face? Where had I seen that face? Where?*

"But, of course, old Horace doesn't care if we don't
get cable. He likes this old junk, don't you, stupid?"
Nora kicked my rump.

By now I was an inch from the TV. *Was he . . .*

"Not so close, Horace, you'll ruin your eyes," Mom
said.

I'd lost him! He'd run out of bullets and ducked behind the stagecoach. *C'mon! Get up! Here comes the
cavalry!*

"What do you know? That's John Wayne, my good-
ness!" Mom said as the big officer in the lead hopped off
his horse.

"Looks like they're all dead!" he said in a solemn
voice from the depths of his diaphragm.

"No, they're not!" I hollered back at the set. "The
driver's alive. The arrow only got his hat."

"Horace is sick, Mom."

I pounded my knees as John Wayne strolled over to
the stagecoach. I wanted him to go to the other side.
Good! He was doing it! Crouching down and giving the
driver a little shake to bring him to his senses.

"Howdy, pardner, yer safe now. The U.S. Cavalry is
here."

"Uhhh . . . what? Huh? Uhh . . ." the poor driver
moaned.

Then there was a close-up. His eyes bugged. "Whar
ma bleedin' from?" he bellowed.

"It is him! It's him! It's him! It's him! I knew it. I knew it! The old guy in the green rocker." I was jumping up and down, clapping. "Yippee!"

Nora crouched behind Mom's chair and peered out. "I mean it, Mom. Horace is mental. He should be locked up."

Eighteen

Something strange was going on at the Wartzburg. When J.D., George, and I arrived for work the next day, the watchman was posted outside the gate, nervously pacing the sidewalk, waiting for us. "Get in that guardhouse! Right now!" he ordered. "And make it snappy changing. Reporters are here."

"Reporters for what?" said J.D.

"To interview Miss Orient. Didn't you fleabags listen to the news this morning? She made a breakthrough in the arson story."

We thought he was pulling our legs till we'd shed our itchy, smelly disguise gear and were heading up the porch steps. "Hey! Look over there," George said, pointing to two blue vans parked outside the delivery entrance. "They're from WQVX-TV. I'll be damned . . . maybe she does know something."

The three of us raced inside, looking for Freddy and Slick. "What's up? What's Pearl's scoop?" we asked when we found them compacting garbage in the kitchen.

"Scoop?" said Slick, looking disgusted. "Man, all she did was draw a sketch of that freak you guys saw on the subway. Y'know? The big mother with the Mohawk? The one who threw the firecracker?"

Freddy nodded. "Then she ran her mouth off, claiming she had inside info on all the punk girls."

"Where'd she get it?" said J.D.

"From nowhere! She just said what George's been saying all along . . . that the punks are part of an organization. They burn stuff to throw the cops off. Keep them from catching the big fish."

"So who called in the press? The cops?"

"No, *estúpido! Pearl* did. Says she's starting a Save The Bronx crusade."

They were really griped. Using George's mastermind theory as her own, Pearl had called the *Daily News* and three local radio reporters. That was *before* breakfast. After breakfast, she'd "leaked" her story to *The New York Times*. By noon, when Freddy and Slick were mowing lawns, she'd stood on the porch, laying a real tearjerker on Rita Maloney, Channel Ten's Roving Eye.

"She woulda made ya barf," said Freddy. "Lookin' at the camera with her big fake crocodile tears, telling Rita how poor old defenseless folks were scared to go to sleep at night. Afraid somebody was gonna burn 'em in their beds."

"I suppose lots of people *are* scared," I said.

"Oh, bull, Ace! Think Pearl cares? She's just doing this for publicity."

And boy, was she getting it. In the few minutes we'd been at the Wartzburg, the phones hadn't stopped ringing. Miss Otterbridge, looking like a veteran track-and-field star, was in constant motion, flying back and forth from room to room, keeping up with her switchboard.

"Please keep your voices down," she said once when she passed us. "They're shooting *Faces-in-the-News* live, up in the sun-room."

"Can we watch?" I asked.

She sighed. "I don't know why not. Everybody else is."

We crowded in next to Flora and Gayle, who were

with a little group behind the piano, about ten feet back
from the lights and cameras. We'd missed the lead-in.
Jerry Orlando, the show's host and New York's top-
ranking gossip, had already made the introductions.
Now he and Pearl were sitting on a couch together,
chatting. She was dressed in about four hundred yards
of pink ruffles and had her hair fixed like a wasp's nest.

"This could be us," Slick whispered. "Right now.
With everybody watching."

"Yeah, dope. Including the Piranhas," said George.

They clammed up when a woman on the crew shot
them a dirty look. Then we all watched the camera-
man. He was zooming in for a close-up of the black-and-
white ink sketch that Pearl held proudly against her
bosom—the punk with the Mohawk.

"Tell us, Miss Orient," Orlando was saying, "what
prompted someone like you—a famous Ziegfeld Follies
girl and former silent film star—to become involved in
a crusade to fight arson?"

Pearl patted a yellow spit curl and smiled. "My re-
cent death."

"*Death?*" Orlando seemed to choke. "Did you say
death?"

"That's right, honey. I died in a subway fire . . . two
weeks ago last Saturday."

Someone was tapping my arm. I turned and saw poor
frazzled Miss Otterbridge trying to reach around the
piano to hand me a note. I was wanted on the phone.

I raced downstairs, thinking, Nuts! Mom's found my
Gravity Guide System again. Why'd I keep forgetting
to return it?

But surprise, surprise. Jerry-as-in-dairy Cone was on
the line. "Howyadoin', there, sweetheart," he bellowed
into my ear. "Long time no speaky, eh? But like I al-

ways told you boys, ya stick with me and I'll land ya a biggie, right? Okay. Now take down this number: 942-1138. Got it? 942-1138."

"Whose is it?" I asked.

"*Whose?* One of the biggest wheels in Hollywood, that's whose! Myron Evans, Jr., head of properties for Global Studios. Just blew into town and wants to set up a meeting with you."

"Jeez! You mean *the* Myron Evans, Jr.?" I screamed. "He's famous! What's he got? A part in a movie for me?"

"Well, now, he wouldn't say precisely. You know how those Hollywood moguls are. Everything's always gotta be top secret. My bet is he's got something hot he wants you to star in. Wouldn't that be something, now?"

"Whew, yeah. Really something."

After I'd hung up, I wondered how a man like Evans knew Cone was my agent. Oh, well. Word does get around. Anyway, it wasn't important.

942-1138. My finger wobbled dialing. Here I go getting shaky, I thought. Constantly nervous.

"Hullo," said a gruff voice. Other voices were in the background. Probably Evans's groupies.

"Yes, I'd like to speak with Myron Evans, Jr., please."

"Who's calling?"

"Oh, uh, Ace. Ace Hobart. And to whom am I speaking?"

"Whom? His secretary."

"Oh, of course, ha-ha. Well, um, would you just tell Mr. Evans I'm on the line? My agent said he wanted to meet me."

"Hold on." He clamped his hand over the mouthpiece, then was back on a few seconds later to tell me Evans was temporarily "indisposed." "But he says

you're to meet him tonight at eight. And *no* agent! Got that? It's private."

"Oh, yes, yes. Of course. Certainly. That's how I like to conduct my own, ha-ha, business. By the way, did he say exactly *where* I should meet him?"

Old Gruff Voice told me to grab a pencil and write down the following:

Reservations for eight at the Garden Room *(Wow! That sounded swank!),* which was on the ground floor of the Starlight Hotel *(Man! First class all the way!)* located at 764 Townsend Street—

"Excuse me, where's Townsend?" I interrupted. "Off Park Avenue? *No?* Oh, I see." *(Incredible!)* "Certainly, I understand . . . Evans likes to keep a low profile. Hates Manhattan. Sure, that's fine. I'll be there."

I hung up. Well, how about that, I thought. There *were* posh places in the Bronx.

What a day! What luck was blowing my way! I took the stairs three at a time back up to the sun-room, curious to see what was happening on *Faces in the News.*

"That's such an inspiring story," I heard Orlando saying as I tiptoed in. "And I hope you don't mind my asking you this, Miss Orient. But when you declined Mr. Pinza's offer to join him in Paradise, was it, well . . . because you believed you were needed on earth? That you had a special destiny to fulfill?"

Pearl dabbed her eyes with a lacy hankie. "Yes, that's right," she sniffed. "I knew I had a mission. And the moment my spirit floated back into my body and I became alive again, I knew what it was. To catch those arsonists!"

The camera lingered awhile on her face, then moved

to Orlando. He leaned forward, smiling gently. "Miss Orient, you're such a vibrant personality . . ."

"Yes, go on."

". . . don't you think it's time your fans talked you out of retirement?"

"Retirement? I never was retired!" she snapped. "I just haven't read any scripts that appealed to me lately."

I glanced at my watch. Now was a good time to tell Miss Otterbridge I needed to leave work an hour early; something I planned to do in complete privacy. Even the Falcons weren't going to hear about my meeting with Evans. Nope, not till tomorrow. *After* I'd signed my movie contract.

Odd. Miss Otterbridge wasn't in her office when I went downstairs. She'd left her switchboard buzzing, shut the door, and disappeared. I scoured the front porch, side patio, and searched in the parlor and dining room. Finally I found her sitting on the little back staircase off the kitchen. She looked bad. Awful. Like she'd just crawled across Death Valley.

"You okay?" I asked.

She shifted her ice bag and rolled her eyes at me, saying, "Fine. Fine. I'll be fine," then slugged down a glass of fizzing Bromo Seltzer.

"You work much, much too hard, Miss Otterbridge. You could use some time off."

"True. True. I do and I could. But the show must go on, as they say."

"Incidentally, speaking of time off . . ."

She was a real good sport about it. She didn't ask me any nosy questions about where I was going, or anything. She just said an hour early was fine.

I thanked her, thinking what a wonderful mother she would've made some lucky kid. Then, just as I started walking into the kitchen, she called me back, telling me I'd be missing an important announcement later.

"It concerns our annual Dramafest," she said, squooshing her ice bag directly onto her right eye. "For forty-six years it's been held religiously on the fourth Saturday in November."

"Oh, yes, I know. Sir Cecil calls it the Wartzburg Renaissance. He says it takes months and months of preparation . . . that every room here explodes with activity! Tired minds turn into quicksilver. Old bodies into . . . *Miss Otterbridge?*"

She'd slumped against the handrail.

"Can I get you something?"

She shook her head, staring into space. "It's been rescheduled," she said. "Twenty-nine days from now . . . the last weekend in August. The board of directors voted on it this morning. It's to perk up morale . . . make up for the outings we've canceled . . ." Her voice trailed.

"Another Bromo Seltzer, maybe?"

"And I've been appointed chairman again," she said, suddenly plunging the ice bag onto her left eye. "Everyone who wants to, participates. They can sing, dance, give a reading, be in a play, direct, prompt, help with costumes, makeup, lighting. Flora and Gayle will do the last act of *A Streetcar Named Desire* . . . it's their seventeenth year. *But* . . ." She paused, looking up at me. "Sir Cecil is breaking his annual tradition. He's giving up Shakespeare to do *Cyrano*. It's for you, Horace. He says you were made for the role."

"That's very kind of him," I said. What else could I say? That there was a big possibility I'd be leaving for

Hollywood soon? That her switchboard was buzzing? I couldn't. Not in her condition.

"Then you'll accept?"

"Well, I . . . uh. I'll definitely consider it."

Nineteen

The name was painted in bold block letters running vertically down the side of the six-story building. STARLIGHT HOTEL, it said. Below the *L* a red arrow pointed to a restaurant entrance on street level.

I slowed down, panting. I'd run all the way from the Wartzburg and now I had to collect myself. It wouldn't look good to barge in, sweaty and breathless, to greet a head honcho from Global Studios.

Myron Evans, Jr. Wow! Was he inside already, watching me? Better act cool, I thought. I used my hand to slick back my hair, shrugged, and pretended to read the menu taped to the Garden Room window. Then I almost laughed. What a deception! From the outside, looking in at the mound of moth carcasses caked on the sill, you'd think the place was a real dive. Hardly an "in" spot for jet-setters.

Eight o'clock on the button, my watch said. I took a breath, commanding myself to walk in and look for a guy in a white Hollywood suit and Yves Saint Laurent shades. And *glow* while you introduce yourself, I added. Charisma's what stars need. It's the chief ingredient for success, says Nevada Culhane. "The gods bestow those who glow." His motto.

Go! Glow! Walk! Talk!

I entered.

"Got a reservation?" said the cashier, a girl in a low-cut yellow blouse, munching peanuts.

"Yes, for eight. But, uh . . ." I looked around. There

wasn't a plant anywhere. "I think I'm in the wrong place. I'm looking for the Garden Room."

"You're in it," she said. "And if your name's Ace, Evans is in the back." Her thumb went up, motioning toward a booth.

In return, I gave her my most glowing, charismatic movie star smile. "Thanks, sugar."

"Spook!" she answered.

No plants. No customers, either. Except for Evans, the Garden Room was empty. Almost. One lone woman was sitting at the counter, eating what appeared to be batter-fried mice. I headed for the back, ignoring the greasy smells coming from the kitchen, and stepped over a pile of floor debris. "Excuse me, sir," I said to the stooped old man who was waiting with his dustpan to sweep it up.

Evans couldn't see me. He had a menu covering his face. Smart, I thought. Real smart. Privacy and business were his first priorities. Not gourmet food.

I slid into the booth, sitting across from him. Apparently he was going incognito. He had on a green T-shirt and his bare brown arms were studded with taut muscles. I liked him already. For a middle-aged mogul, he really kept in shape.

"Ah-hemmm," I said to let him know I'd arrived.

He lowered the menu in a movement as smooth as pulling down a window shade. I stared at his face, gasping, not knowing whether to bolt or scream. "Sit!" he hissed. Then one strong hand shot across the table, grabbing my wrist.

I'd been had. "Stab," I squeaked. "*Stab* Evans!"

"Figured tricking you was the only way I'd get you in here," he said. I wanted to cry. His pincers were sinking

into my wristbones. "You wouldn't've come otherwise, right?"

I quickly glanced around, expecting Cannibal or one of the other Piranhas to spring out from the shadows, brandishing a switchblade.

Stab guessed what I was thinking. "I came alone," he said. "Just like my man on the phone said I would. Thought it was time you and me had a nice, friendly talk. Face-to-face, like this." With that, he released my wrist.

"Why didn't you pick Freddy Cruz? He's the Falcon leader."

Stab smiled. "Cannibal and Turtle and me decided you'd be better. You seem more with it. Know what I mean? Like you got lots"—his smile got bigger—"of smarts."

I felt flattered and smiled back. "How'd you know Jerry Cone was my agent?"

He reached for a toothpick lying next to a used napkin. "Simple," he said, digging crud out of one of his molars. "I pick up the phone, call your house, and your sister tells me."

"Either of you two decided yet?"

Both of us looked up at our waiter. He was the same old stooped guy who'd been sweeping up garbage. And naturally he hadn't washed his hands. The stuff caked under his nails looked like the veiny gunk Mom used to clean out of shrimp. (Back in the days when we could afford shrimp.)

"The tab's on me. Order anything you want," Stab said, pushing the menu at me.

"Oh, no. I couldn't."

"Yeah, I mean it. Order! Cuchifritos, fritters, fries, chili dogs, anything."

"Let's see," I said, pretending to study today's specials. But I'd already decided. I'd order the only meal Uncle Jake ever ate when he traveled to Calcutta. It saved him from dysentery while he was in the merchant marine.

"Gimme two Sloppy Joes with double slops and a triple egg cream. The best in the house," Stab told the waiter.

"Let's see," I said again. "I'll have a cup of hot tea. Very hot. Make sure the water's boiling. And a boiled egg. *Hard*-boiled." My stomach growled. "In fact, make it three boiled eggs."

Stab gave me a queer look. "You kidding?"

"No, no . . . that's it. Doctor's orders. I've got an albumin deficiency."

Our waiter looked at Stab and shrugged. "All types come in here," he said.

While we were waiting to be served, Stab came right out and asked me bluntly why the Falcons hadn't stayed in Bermuda. "What happened? You guys get canned?"

"Canned? Naw, we didn't like Brookie," I lied. "Too tall. Whines all the time . . . her mother's always with her. We quit."

He smiled. "So what's this other movie you've been filming?"

"Other movie?"

His smile disappeared. "Look," he said, leaning across the table, "if we're gonna keep this friendly, we need to level with each other, okay? I wanna hear about this other flick! We know you're in it."

My hands were getting clammy. What on earth was

he talking about? "You mean the"—I was about to take a gamble—"flick we're doing at the Wartzburg?"

"That's right. Cannibal and me see you going up there in drag every day. They paying you a lot?"

"Oh, not a lot. A little. It's sort of for charity . . . a fund-raiser. The Wartzburg needs money."

"Yeah? They'd have to pay me a million bucks to dress up in those crapola bag-lady costumes you been wearing. You got a dumb agent, y'know that?" He examined the crud he'd just dug out of his tooth. "I need a root canal," he said. "But I ain't getting one. Unless they put me to sleep." He dropped the toothpick into an ashtray and looked up. "So what's the movie's plot? Some kind of comedy?"

On the spot I started making up a story about a demented old woman who thinks her fellow residents in an old folks home are trying to do her in. "One by one she knocks them off," I said. "Poison. Strangulation. Pushing them down the stairs. The usual."

"Who plays the woman?" Stab asked. "That fat broad who was crying on Rita Maloney's show this morning? Pearl Orient?"

I nodded.

"And who're you? A detective? Dressed up like an old slob in order to get inside to nail her?" He kept asking questions and I kept nodding. "Sounds dumb," he said.

Our waiter was slamming our orders on the table. "Boiled four minutes," he said as he put the eggs under my nose.

"What about my tea?"

"Same. Boiled four minutes. Luigi made it with the egg water."

As I lifted the tea bag out of the cup, Stab finished half

his egg cream in one guzzle. "Tell me more about this broad Pearl Orient," he said. "Which one of you Falcons helped her figure out there was an arson organization? George?"

"Oh, none of us did. I swear, Stab. Pearl's smart. Real smart. Figured it all out by herself. Didn't need *no*body . . . ha-ha . . . to help her."

"Then tell her thanks from us Piranhas."

"Thanks?" I was so surprised, I took a big sip of tea without thinking and scalded my tongue. "But why? I thought the punk girls were your girl friends."

He bit into a Sloppy Joe. "You sick in the head, man? We *hate* those mothers! Best thing that ever happened in the Bronx . . . them getting thrown in the slammer. Hope a judge lets 'em rot there."

"One's still on the loose," I said. "The freak with the Mohawk."

"Bunny? Naw. Cops picked her up tonight. Caught her hiding out in the Model Youth Center. Lady who runs the place recognized her."

He sounded too sincere to be putting me on. But I had to make sure. "If you hated them all so much, why'd you hang out with them?"

"Wasn't no choice of ours. They're ex-*tort*ionists! Been up-surping our turf all year. Taking *our* money."

U-surping I wanted to say. Instead I cracked my eggshells and decided to test him further. "Too bad nobody's nailed their ringleader, huh?"

Stab got a funny smile on his face. "That's one of the reasons I wanted us to meet . . . to tell you something." He swatted a small gray moth off his plate, then leaned toward me, whispering. "There's a reward posted for information leading to his arrest. Ten thousand bucks, we heard."

I whistled. "You know who he is?"

"Shhh!"

"Man, if you know, why aren't you collecting?"

His beady eyes darted in the direction of the cashier. "Too risky, understand? Us Piranhas would get our throats slit."

"Pearl didn't get hers slit for running her mouth off."

"That's *her*. We're us! Nobody's gonna fool with an old broad. Say!" He thought a minute. "I got an idea."

"Yeah?" I was hoping it was the same idea I had.

"Why don't I tell you, you tell Pearl, then *she* can go to the police?"

"And make her agree to split the ten-grand reward with you?"

His eyes darted toward the cashier again. "Naw. Still too risky. The money's gonna have to be *all* Pearl's. Us Piranhas can't be involved in any way anyone can pin on us."

I swallowed, thinking this was going to be the easiest five thousand the Falcons ever made. Pearl would have to split with *us*.

"See this? The ringleader's name's written on it," Stab said, pulling a crumpled piece of paper out of his pocket. "The guy's a big slumlord. Owned some of them buildings that was burned down . . . paid plenty to have it done so he could collect megabucks in insurance."

I reached for the paper. "How'd you know about him?"

"Hey! Now hold it!" Stab's hand came crashing down on mine, nearly fracturing four of my fingers. "How do I know you won't use this to collect the money yourself?"

"Who? *Me?* Deprive an old lady?" I blew on my sting-

ing fingers. "Besides, I don't want to get *my* throat slashed."

He drummed his nails on the table. "Hmm. Tell ya what. How's about you paying me twenty bucks for the name? I'll give the twenty to Cannibal . . . his poor little sister's in the hospital. Needs an eye operation. When Pearl collects the reward, she'll give you back the twenty."

"I only got twelve bucks with me," I said. "And I need one to get home."

"Okay, gimme eleven bucks," he said.

Actually, I had more. I had twelve-fifty plus a subway token. But I didn't tell Stab, because I planned on using the extra change to make a few phone calls once I got to Grand Central.

The whole ride down there, I kept staring at the name that was going to make each of us Falcons a thousand bucks: Bob Garsen. It made me laugh. Who ever would've thought somebody with a sweetie-pie name like Bob could be a mean, merciless arson mastermind? Not me. I'd expected somebody who sounded sinister. Like F.B. for Flesh Burner.

Stab had even written down Garsen's Manhattan office address. Man, oh, man, was this a goodie. Maybe not as good as getting a Global Studios contract—I wasn't deluding myself—but boy, it was close.

When I got off the train at 42nd Street, my spirits were on the outer fringes of the stratosphere. Ace, you're a clever son of a gun, I thought as I headed for the nearest pay phone.

I had five calls to make: home, the Rising Star Talent Agency, the Bronx 50th Police Precinct, then to Raven and George. In that order.

Home was first because I didn't want Mom to worry. I simply lied and told her I was working a little late and not to expect me till ten-thirty. Call completed.

I dug in my pocket for more change. This next call was going to give me a thrill of a lifetime. I dialed. 555-9310. Of course I knew Jerry Cone wouldn't be in this late. Didn't matter. Leaving him a message was satisfying enough. Ringing.

"Hello, this is a recording. You have reached the Rising Star Talent Agency, the place where galactic superstars are born. No one is available to speak with you at this hour, but if you would care to leave a message, please do so after the following beep."

I waited. *Beep.* I took a deep breath. "The following message is for Jerry-as-in-dairy Cone," I said. Pause. "Why, hello there, sweetheart. This is *Ace*-as-in-space *Hobart*-as-in-go-stick-your-head-in-a-bucket! I suppose you want to know what happened at my meeting with Myron Evans, Jr., huh? You'll never know. As of this moment, you no longer represent the astounding talents of the Purple Falcons, who are as follows: Yours Truly, Federico Cruz, George Wyciewski, Tony "Slick" Vaccaro, and J.D. Jackson. You're fired, ya bum! *Ta-dummm!* Don't call us. We won't call you. *Tooodle-ooo!*"

I hung up, grinning. Should've done that weeks ago. From now on there'd be one less bite out of our hard-earned paychecks.

Forward. On to bigger and better things. The call to the Bronx 50th Police Precinct. I rubbed the coin in my hand, thinking about the reward money. Five thousand for Pearl, five thousand for . . . Hey! *Why should Pearl get half?*

"Better wait in line for another phone," I said to the

man in the gray business suit who was standing behind me. "I'm going to be a while."

Absolutely no privacy in these places. Not since they tore out the glass booths and put in these stand-up stalls. Now, what'd I been thinking? Oh, yeah. About Pearl. Well, sorry, you old witch. But tonight I'm working exclusively for the Falcons. And we're going to split ten thousand, *five* ways.

I put in my money and dialed 911, the police emergency number. "Please connect me with the Bronx Fiftieth," I told the switchboard operator. "This is extremely urgent."

A minute later I was talking to a Sergeant Hanover. "I'd like to speak with the captain," I said. "I have vital information concerning the Bronx arson"—Crap! That businessman was still behind me—"uh, mastermind," I finished in a whisper.

"Gimme your name," said Sergeant Hanover.

"Ace Hobart. H-o-b-a-r-t."

"The number you're calling from?"

"763-9682. It's a pay phone."

"Speak a little louder, would you? I can't hear you."

I did. And this time I gave him my home number.

"Okay. Now what're you reporting?"

"Vital information concerning the Bronx arson mastermind," I repeated. "I want to give it to the captain."

"Sorry, the captain's unavailable."

"Look! I've gotta talk to the *captain!*"

"All calls go through me, understand? So if you'll just state your information."

We argued, but he wouldn't give in. I had to. "Got a pencil?" I asked.

"Typewriter."

"Okay. The guy you're looking for is a slumlord.

Owner of some of the buildings that were burned down recently in the Bronx. He paid the arsonists to do it. The motive was to collect insurance."

"Go on."

"Well, his name is Bob Garsen. G-a-r-s-e-n. And his Manhattan office address is number One Broadway. Got all that?" I asked.

There was a hoot loud enough to break my eardrum. "Hey, Baroni, we got another prankster," Hanover hollered to somebody. "This one you won't believe." Then to me he said, "Okay, kid. Who put you up to this?"

I was outraged. "This is no prank!" I snapped. "The arson mastermind you're looking for is Bob Garsen. G-a-r-s-e-n!"

"Good try, kid. Very funny. Nobody's ever pulled our leg about the New York City Police Commissioner before," Hanover said over volleys of laughter. "You even got the address for his headquarters straight."

I hung up and stared at the phone like it was a double-barreled shotgun.

"You finished your calls yet?" asked the businessman behind me.

Twenty

I walked home. I was too poor for subway rides. My last eighty-five cents had to be conserved for tomorrow—payday.

Idiot! Moron! Jackass! I punched myself. Kicked myself on the shin. At that moment the Piranhas were probably sitting on a Bronx stoop laughing themselves senseless. They'd set me up. Stab knew, just knew, I'd fall for the reward gag. Robert Garsen. The New York City Police Commissioner. Of course he was! I'd been so money-hungry, I hadn't recognized his name.

Imbecile! Jerk! That eleven bucks I'd shelled out had paid for Stab's Sloppy Joes! Even my own X*&#D1/4#*Z*X eggs.

Lucky for me, the next day we were so busy, none of the Falcons thought to ask why I'd left work early the night before. And I wasn't about to volunteer the truth.

Raven and I went out for Cokes and fries that evening and I didn't tell her, either. If anyone found out, I'd confess. Otherwise my gullible role in the Piranha con game was going to the grave with me, unknown.

She and I were sitting across from each other at a butcher-block table in Lenny's Beef, a joint near her apartment building. While I was telling her the news from the Wartzburg, I was practicing the stuff Sir Cecil had been hammering into me all week: *Observation.* He calls it the Fifth Great Lesson of Acting.

"So that's what all the hustle and bustle's about these days at the Wartzburg. The Dramafest. Arson's a dead topic!" I said, wrenching my gaze from Raven's shining face to observe the waiter's walk. As he came toward us with our order, I noticed a rolling gait and a little click of the left knee that made him wince. He slapped the tray down on the table and dealt out the food and drinks.

"Whaddya starin' at, fella?" he said, and left.

"Ace, that's rude," Raven whispered. "You're not supposed to stare at people, especially funny-looking ones. He's likely to knock your block off."

"I am so supposed to," I whispered back. "Sir Cecil's teaching me to concentrate, to see the nuances of human behavior and to develop a *memory bank* of behaviors. When I need some—"

"Why are you whispering?"

"Oh. I guess I was observing you and imitating you back." (Was I! I was trying to see her reactions and read her unspoken signs.) "When I need something for a character in a play, then I'll have it in my memory bank. He's training me to be an actor from the inside out, not to just pretend on stage. . . ."

Raven, sipping her Coke, was nodding her head in understanding.

"Sir Cecil told me that if you want to know if somebody cares about you deeply, all you've got to do is to observe the pupils of their eyes. If they dilate, looking at you, then they're fascinated."

Raven giggled and closed her eyes. "I'm not going to let you see mine, then."

"I already know about you," I said with total confidence. It was pure acting, stolen from the cop who told me that Robert Garsen was the police commissioner.

I think I fooled Raven. She leaned forward like she expected something else in that tough-guy, sure-of-myself style. "You do?" she said, looking at me over the rim of her glass.

I leaned forward, too, but didn't have anything to say, so I leaned a little farther and tried to kiss her.

She reeled back in her seat. "We're in public!" she said.

"So?"

"I don't like to kiss in public places," she hissed.

"I know that," I said, trying to recoup the confidence she seemed to like. But the words came out whiny. Pure Flora de Flor!

There was a sticky, quiet moment.

"Well, what are they doing for the Dramafest and where's it being held?" she said, not sounding mad anymore.

"A whole bunch of stuff. Two old vaudeville actors are resurrecting a slapstick routine. Somebody's juggling. PeeWee wants to accompany J.D. doing a little soft-shoe routine. Then there will be film clips from old movies starring Whar Ma Bleedin' From, Pearl, and Miss Belva Bithell. Before tea today, Miss Otterbridge announced over the intercom, " 'Actors and actresses . . .' " I said, imitating her voice. " 'You will be pleased to know that scenes from four plays have been selected. You'll find the available parts listed on the bulletin board outside my office.' "

Raven clapped her hands and her eyes sparkled. "You sound just like she did when I spoke with her on the phone!"

"Yeah?"

"It's great!"

"Huh! Well, I've been observing *her*, too. The twiggy

ladies," I continued, "are doing *A Streetcar Named Desire* for the seventeenth year. They cast themselves as the southern sisters Stella and Blanche. Their notice said all they're looking for is a handsome, muscular, sexy, coarse, and rather dim-witted-looking man to play Stanley."

Raven gave me a questioning look, but I shook my head.

"Their first choice was Freddy. He turned them down. He wants to be the stage manager and build the sets. Then they asked Slick, who told them flatly he'd be too busy choreographing his own original ballet and break-dancing solo."

"Wow!" Raven said.

"Then Sir Cecil surpris—"

"*He's* not going to play Stanley, the Marlon Brando part. Not that old man!"

"No, of course not."

"Well, who is?"

"They're not sure yet. But Sir Cecil surprised everybody by breaking his annual Shakespearean tradition and announcing he's directing *Cyrano de Bergerac,* an old French play."

"You're in that one?"

"I don't know . . ." I said, shaking my head.

"Well, what's the matter?" Raven said.

"Sir Cecil took me down to the basement to look at the theater. Miss Otterbridge was there too, showing everybody else around. It's called the Barrymore Little Theater and it's beautiful . . . George went wild over the lighting equipment. Alfonso's going to teach him how to use it. Slick liked the stage floor for dancing . . . some kind of soft wood. George is going to be the sound director, too. . . ."

"But what about you?" Raven said.

"I don't know. Sir Cecil's told me he wants me to play Cyrano, but when I stood up on stage with the foot-lights shining in my eyes, I didn't feel excited anymore. Here he's been working with me every day and when I stood up there, it just didn't appeal to me."

Raven looked suspicious.

"Isn't that a blast? After all Sir Cecil's efforts, and my blabbing to Mom and everybody about wanting so bad to be an actor, I don't care about it at all!" I said.

Raven's eyebrows wrinkled into little silky ribbons. "Ace, I can't believe that."

I looked down and ate a couple french fries and took another sip of Coke. But I'd lost my appetite.

When the waiter brought the check, I insisted on paying. Raven protested, but I had to do some little thing for her. We got up and walked out. She was the first person I'd told about my doubts. I thought I'd feel relieved. Instead I felt rotten.

We went straight home. She had to shrink-wrap a lot of chicken for a sale at Gristede's the next day. They wanted her early.

Walking up the stairs inside her building, she took my hand. "Ace, when you were standing on that stage," she said gently, "you may have felt scared. Did you think of that?"

"I didn't feel scared!" I dropped her hand.

She laughed. "You've never heard of stage fright?"

"There wasn't a play going on," I snapped. "How could I have been afraid?"

"Oh . . . oh. Okay . . ." she said, but a question hung in the air.

At the top of the stairs near the door to her apart-

ment, she said, "Your mom's so nice to me during lunch breaks . . ."

"You mean you *like* eating with her?" I said nervously.

"But during store hours she doesn't say one word. She's a serious worker. You take after her. Maybe that's why you're feeling a little . . . hesitant about doing the part. Like your mom, you're very serious about things."

"I am?"

She nodded, reaching out and touching my cheek.

I had to turn away. I wanted her to think I was strong and passionate. She was making me feel uncomfortable and dumb.

"I gotta go," I said as she took her key out.

"Ace? Will you call me up as soon as you decide what you're going to do about the part?"

I nodded.

"Promise?" she said.

"Sure, sure, sure." I spun around and headed down the steps. Tomorrow first thing, I thought, I'm going to sign up to be an usher.

"Good night, Ace! Thanks for the Coke!" Raven called after me. I heard the door close.

Well, at least I didn't have to wear the bag-lady stuff anymore, thanks to Stab. He'd freed me from that bondage. And I never have to wear my eyepatch again either. I wasn't going to be an actor.

Knowing that, riding up to work the next morning, felt so good. I was free!

Telephone repairmen and Gristede's cashiers don't have actors for kids. Where'd I get that idea anyway? If

I was in a play, Nora would find out. And come! I couldn't have that.

Once in my old high school in Guttenberg, N.J., a guy got so nervous doing *Annie Get Your Gun* that he wet his pants on stage. And he was a football player.

My bladder isn't so great. I wouldn't want to trust it. Gee, maybe I *was* scared!

Sir Cecil's daughter visited him at the Wartzburg that afternoon. He had to cancel our acting lesson. What a break! I dreaded telling him that I wasn't doing the part. He'd put a lot into me. It might break him up. Give him an early death.

At dinner, to avoid him, I offered to feed Belva Bithell and Whar Ma Bleedin' From, although it was not my turn. J.D., who hated the job, happily accepted. Then Sir Cecil got up from his table on the other side of the dining room and left before I'd even finished giving the old folks their salads. Was I relieved!

But then George came by and dropped a note in my lap. "Here. Sir Cecil asked me to give this to you."

It was written in beautiful script on cream-colored notepaper with his initials. *Dear Ace,* it said. *Before you leave tonight, please pick up your script in my room. Start memorizing the lines right away. It's a long part.*

When I got home, Raven was on the phone.

"You're just in time, Horace," Mom said, handing over the receiver. I didn't know how long they'd been talking.

"I'll get it in my room," I said.

"Well, did you make up your mind?" Raven said as soon as I picked up.

"Hang up, Mom!" I shouted. Then when I heard the click finally, I said, "Sure."

"Well, what?"

"I didn't want to do it, Raven. Honestly. But I don't know what it is. I just couldn't say no."

"That's just what I thought would happen!"

"You did?"

"Yes, Ace, I knew it." She sounded so happy.

"Knew what?"

"That you're hooked. That's all. If it hooks you . . . Acting. Then you can't say no. That's all there is to it."

Nora looked up from the Young Love Romance she was reading while watching the Saturday-morning cartoons. "What are you doing reading that book and whispering to yourself? Ace? *Ace?* ACE!"

"What, what?"

"I'm asking you for the tenth time, what you're d—"

"Learning computer language."

I read the line again that I'd been trying to memorize since eleven o'clock.

Nora cut off the TV and stood up. "You can't act," she said.

I riveted my attention on the page, shielding it from her nosy view, and listened for her to walk out.

There was no movement, though, in the coffin-quiet of the Hobart living room. Just the ticking of the old Regulator measuring the two hours left into hundreds of little splinters. I didn't have the whole part memorized, and after dishes tonight at the Wartzburg we were having a full rehearsal. We'd been practicing the play for almost *two weeks* now. I studied my long speeches every night. *Cyrano*'s a hundred-year-old French play. The language is tough!

"I said you can't be an actor."

I ignored the brat, the pug, the knob, the buttonhead . . .

"You're my brother and I feel you should know that

you'll never be an actor. I'm not saying it mean, you nincompoop!"

Ticktick. Ticktick. Ticktick went the clock.

"In the movie they told you what to do every minute. You were believable as the kid who gets killed under the hoop. I mean, you are a kid. But that's not exactly acting. Acting is when you bury your own self, and become another person. . . ."

I raised an eyelid to look at Einstein.

"In another place, an imaginary place. You have to, um . . . um, what do they call it?" She squinched her eyes closed.

"Empathize?" I shot out.

"In . . . in . . . interpret. Interpret! You can't interpret a character in a play, because you don't even know yourself, much less another character. To be an actor, you have to express real emotions for a fake person."

Ticktick. Ticktick. Ticktick.

"I mean it. You'll never be an actor!"

I catapulted out of the chair and grabbed her by the hair. The script went flying to the floor. "You're full of . . . of . . . Just because you haven't seen me act yet doesn't mean a thing. It's you who don't know who I am. It's you who are dumb, too stupid to know an actor when you live with one. I've always been an actor. I'm a born actor."

I took a breath from the diaphragm, using Sir Cecil's technique, and continued. "You think you know about acting? You don't even know the name of one teenage actor on Broadway. . . ."

"Yes I do. Matthew Broderick."

"Anyway, I can play all kinds of parts, different people, all ages. Why? Because I observe people and know

how they feel inside. Like Paul Newman, I'm a method actor, from the inside out. I could even play Pearl Orient, a big, fat old woman. I know who she is and who she wants to be. Those things not meshing give her all kinds of trouble and unhappiness. I can do her walk because I've watched her move with fake grace and real hostility."

"Let go. You're hurting. *Dad!*"

"No." I said, softening my hold but not letting go. "It's your turn. You won't listen to anybody unless they pin you down and make you. You're afraid . . . because for once they might be right. And you, wrong."

Nora's eyelashes fluttered.

"But we were talking about me—Ace Hobart, an actor. I'm going to play the part of Cyrano de Bergerac because Sir Cecil Bancroft thinks I can. He's recognized that I, old Horace, the wimp from Guttenberg, can learn the lines, practice the scenes, and *be* Cyrano with his ugly nose . . . even though I, of course, am not really bad-looking."

"Hah," she said, but it was an octave higher than her last words, with question marks in front of the sentence as well as at the end, too.

"And I can say Cyrano's poetic sentences and the audience will believe me even though in real life I talk street talk just like the rest of the Falcons."

"You're not as good as Matt Dillon."

"No, I'm not."

"And you're going to get stage fright and your voice will sound like a bird's chirp. . . ." She yanked herself away from my grip and ran to the other side of the room.

"My voice won't squeak. When I'm scared, it sounds like a foghorn."

Nora grabbed the script and started reading one of the old-fashioned lines. "Here are three . . . six . . . embosomed in a poem by . . . hee-hee! *Embosomed!* You'll never be able to say that in front of people."

I took the line, said it, and showed her.

"Ace, make a bet with me. If you miss one line, you have to give me your water bed, okay? If you don't, I'll give you five dollars." She slowly twisted a ring of her curly hair around a finger.

I stared at her, thinking, You're jealous. That's what it is!

Suddenly she turned and ran out of the room.

"Dad!" she yelled. "Ace is crazy. When he talks, his voice goes *brrrrrrr* like an opera singer's."

Alone at last, I leapt on the only stage in the Hobart apartment, the brown couch, and let myself be transformed into Cyrano. My eyes glinted. I was heavier, older, but even stronger; there was a sword in my hand. I felt myself become this really brave guy who leads the bravest company in the French Guards. Not only fearless, Cyrano's a poet, with a great soul.

Saying my lines out loud, fearless that Nora or Dad would hear (Mom was at Gristede's. She probably would have enjoyed it!), I stabbed the drapes with my imaginary blade and thrust so hard, I slipped off the couch and hit the floor, but—still in character—I rolled over, got up, and continued the speech. It was terrific, I thought.

And then I realized, I had the *whole thing* memorized.

I knew I knew my part.

Yippee!

On the Thursday before Big Saturday, the day of our show, Raven went with me to our old movie location, the park near the East River. I told her it would bring me luck to run my lines there.

So at the crack of dawn she met me in front of her apartment. Since we wanted to run uptown along the river, one of my favorite places, we both wore our jogging suits.

Raven's looked like a movie star's—pink satin with cream stripes. In my gray gym sweats I looked like sludge moving next to her.

When we got there, the park was as scroungy as ever. The early sunlight, though, was sort of shimmery and it speckled the broken concrete under the leafy trees. Raven had brought croissants in her daypack, and juicy oranges.

I'd never had a croissant before. Raven said they were French. Little buttery buns curved like a crescent moon. I bit into one and discovered it had as much bread in it as a fortune cookie.

Raven took little nibbles. "Aren't these yummy?" We were side by side on a bench with cracked slats.

I nodded. Cyrano would have loved them. But my stomach growled. It wanted a Big Mac.

"Have a segment?" she said, opening an orange so the juice squirted. "They're good for performers, vitamin C for stress." She popped one in her mouth and chewed, which made her cheeks rounder and even more satiny.

"Okay!" I said, beginning to think of other things besides practicing the play.

"Come on, Ace . . . we've got to get started," she said softly.

I was just about to make a move on her. Darn! I

handed her the paperback copy of *Cyrano* that I'd
jammed into my sweats pocket. "It's where the paper
clip is; my part's underlined."

"The Bakery of the Poets?"

"Flip over a page, we've cut some out. This is where I
come in." I pointed to the place.

She turned a few pages and looked ahead. "What a
long part. So many speeches, what's it about?"

"Cyrano's this really brave guy that everybody ad-
mires. He leads a company of soldiers. He's not only
fearless, he's a poet. But the trouble is, he's ugly. With a
huge nose like a rhino. He's been in love with Roxane
ever since he was a little kid. She leads him on to think
she loves him back, and then she knocks him for a loop
by telling him she's really mad for Christian, who is hot
for her too. But Christian, who's in Cyrano's company,
the one he leads, isn't good at poetry like Cyrano. Back
then, writing poems to your love was real big like, um
. . . well, you know . . . being romantic is now."

"Yes?" Raven said, looking very seriously into my
eyes.

"So anyway, big-hearted Cyrano agrees to write Roxane poetry for this dude Christian, which makes her fall
in love even more. Really she loves the poet, not the
handsome guy."

"Ohhh. That's nice."

"Yeah!" I looked down and felt kind of sad. "The
thing is, though, they never get to consummate their
love and Cyrano just goes on alone for his life. Not
defeated, but alone."

"That's great!" she said. "But sad, too. Who is pl—"

"You think I can do it? Play Cyrano?" I said, inter-
rupting her.

"Well . . . don't *you?* Doesn't *Sir Cecil?* Let's start."

She began reading off the lines to me. At first it felt dumb and I'd stumble, but then she'd smile and give me the word I'd fluffed and we'd go on. In the middle of the act, she began to read Roxane's part. I really got into it then. I felt my character from the feet up, as Sir Cecil would say. Even Nevada Culhane, my hero, had said, "I can tell an impersonator every time unless he does it from the feet up." I was doing Cyrano that way; I had weights in my shoes to make me feel older. Sir Cecil gave them to me. Running with them this morning had almost got me used to them.

"Tell me what you were going to tell me—if you dared?" I said as Cyrano.

Raven, reading Roxane, answered, "I think I do dare —now. Listen, I love someone."

"Ah!" I said.

"Someone who does not know," Raven said.

"Ah!" I said, in lower pitch.

"At least, not yet."

Raven's voice was teasing. "Ah!" I said again.

"But he will know. Some day," she said. Raven had turned cranberry-red.

I didn't remember my next "Ah!" I just sort of stared at her. Then she giggled.

"Hey, what's wrong?"

She laughed and laughed. She couldn't stop. "Come on, tell me, which one of the old ladies gets to play Roxane?" she said, giggling.

"Oh, it's Jacqueline, one of the housekeepers, you know, an actress."

"Jacqueline! You didn't tell me about her. Who is she?"

"She's this girl. She's about twenty." I told her *that,*

but I didn't tell her that sometimes when I kissed Roxane/Jacqueline in the scene, I really liked it.

"You never mentioned any young woman working at the Wartzburg."

"Huh! Didn't I?"

"No, you didn't!"

"Well . . ."

"Let's finish this. I gotta get home," Raven said. "I gotta get a shower and get to work."

The rest of the rehearsal was kind of a dud. After we finished, we took the bus home. On the way, I told her about the costumes in the Wartzburg attic, how we'd gone up there to get whatever we needed. The collection of stuff was huge! She wanted to know if Jacqueline had gone too. But I skipped answering and said, "Tonight I have to iron the jacket and sew the buttons on. Tomorrow's dress rehearsal."

"I'll come and see it," Raven said.

"I want you to, but not until the performance. You can come Saturday."

"Why not for the dress rehearsal?"

"We're going to do it the best on Saturday. That's what I want you to see."

"But if I came tomorrow night, I could give you some notes after I see it . . . why don't I? It wouldn't be any trouble."

"Well, that's nice. Hey, thanks!"

The bus was pulling up at 23rd Street. A crowd of people was getting on. The morning rush was starting. Suddenly, Raven jumped up. "See you later, Ace. I want to run into the beauty supply store here for something. . . ."

"Oh, I didn't know you were getting off before your stop."

"See you tomorrow!"

"Okay."

And she was gone. But not forgotten! I'm glad I didn't tell her Jacqueline had gone up to the attic. She wouldn't like it if she knew Jackie had tried on and taken off costumes right there in front of everybody. She said that's how they do it in summer stock theaters. Nobody's got time for modesty. It was okay with me. No wonder I want to be an actor!

Twenty-two

"Hey, what's the matter, Ace?" J.D. whispered. "You were highly prosmosigus, why so blue?"

"Pearl told me an old stage motto. '*Bad* dress rehearsal. *Good* opening night.' Except for Slick tonight, we were great!"

"Oh! So does that mean he'll be brilliant tomorrow in the Dramafest and all the rest of us will be a mess?"

"If you can believe Pearl," I said.

For the first time in his life, Slick Vaccaro had been drunk. Rip-roaring, tripping-over-his-dancing-feet drunk. Blotto.

After the dress rehearsal we were taken home in a big yellow Checker cab that Miss Otterbridge treated us to. I was squeezed between Raven and Jacqueline, smooshed like a contented sardine. I hoped we'd never get home! J.D. and George were sitting ahead of us on the fold-down seats that Checkers have. Freddy was next to the driver and could be seen through the bullet-proof glass. He'd just pointed out the latest building to be scorched to ruins in the Bronx. The only good thing that could be said about it was that at least it wasn't near the Wartzburg and the Barrymore Little Theater. Next to Raven, sprawled out and snoring like a granddaddy, was Slick.

The dress rehearsal had gone off without a hitch. Except for Slick. Alfonso set lights and ran them. George on audio played different tapes for each part of

the program and for sound effects. He's found this tweedly music for my play and it sounded just right. Freddy handled props and moved the scenery he and some of the housekeeping lovelies had built and painted. His bakery for Cyrano de Bergerac made me feel like I lived in the seventeenth century, was horny in the seventeenth century. Just think, it happened all through history. And people survived to old age. Raven snuggled a little closer in the cab.

We got to see Pearl in *Wanton Woman,* a film from the thirties. She was good-looking!

I might even have liked her, if I'd been young back then.

It was only as she was electrocuting John Barrymore in the big final scene and screaming and yelling that I could even recognize her as our old girl. The big mouth gave her away.

A Streetcar Named Desire turned out real weird. Flora and Gayle had argued over who got to play Blanche. They couldn't remember who had done it last year. They didn't find an actor to play Stanley, and Gayle ended up doing it to Flora's Blanche! Watching it, we'd laughed so hard, we had to sneak out of the auditorium.

Since my play was longest, they put it in the middle. Jacqueline, whose eyes sparkled as much as if not more than Raven's, was fantastic as Roxane. I really felt in love with her on stage. It was wild. And I did the whole thing without flubbing a line.

Why hadn't I made the bet with Nora?

Because I didn't want her to see us, of course. Nobody at home had a clue that tomorrow was not only the opening night but the closing one, too. One time and no family! That's what I wanted.

Freddy turned around and talked through the money drawer between the front seat and the back. "How'd you learn to soft-shoe so fast?" he asked J.D.

" 'Cause I gots natchral rhythm, Jack."

He sounded like PeeWee all the time.

PeeWee had played a hot and rolling "Take the 'A' Train" by Duke Ellington. Even Miss Otterbridge couldn't sit still during his rendition. It blew the lid right off the fancy Barrymore Little Theater. Everybody was beating their feet against the plush carpet under the cushy seats. Of course, it didn't make a sound.

The Dramafest dress rehearsal had closed with Slick's dancing to "I Don't Want Your Jujubes, Babee!" and messing up on every routine he'd practiced. What a disaster!

Later, when we were taking off our makeup in the dressing room, Sir Cecil wheeled in with his notes and patted me on the back. "Young man, you really did it! My congratulations on the veracity of your characterization."

"Righ-ton!" Slick had said drunkenly.

I was embarrassed by that remark in front of Sir Cecil. He thought so highly of his work. And then, too, Pearl had just told me that awful saying about a bad dress rehearsal meaning a good performance. I dreaded to think what Sir Cecil would say tomorrow if I screwed up. So I couldn't answer when he congratulated me. Even though it meant a lot.

"Ah, my boy, that's right. Keep silent," he said after a moment. "You are no doubt descending from the heights you reached in your performance."

He wheeled himself out without another word.

I pulled off my putty nose and packed it in its little can. Was I depressed.

In the cab an hour later, George turned around and tried to get Slick to explain what had happened to him.

"I don't think he's come to yet, George," Raven said, her hand spread out on my knee, a ring on every finger, polish on every nail. All this time I'd thought being nice was going to get to Raven's protected heart. Why hadn't Dad told me about the effectiveness of the Other Woman? If I ever had a kid, that would be the first thing I'd tell him. But poor Dad, he probably didn't know anything. He was pre-bomb, pre-TV, everything. Jacqueline had just said she was tired and wanted to know if I minded her resting her head on my shoulder. It was all right with me. She could rest anything she wanted!

Raven was pinching me. "Hey, cut it out!" I said.

"Can you stop what you're thinking and listen to Slick?"

I hadn't realized he'd finally come to.

"You're not paying attention to the conversation, stuck-up actor!" Raven said.

"Gimme a break!" How'd she know what I'd been thinking?

"My mother got me drunk," Slick was saying.

"What?" Freddy said through the paybox.

"My mother got me drrunkkkk."

"She did not!" George and J.D. said at the same time.

"Drunkk as a lord."

The cab reached the Triborough Bridge and made a hard right, slinging us all against each other.

"She said that I cannot go to ballet school, or any other fancy-pants things, because I have to start pulling my own train . . . paying my way. Classes are jus' too esspensive." He hiccupped. "They took our TV, our

bumper pool, jus' because I didn't pay the loan. So when she said those things to me, I jus' got out her booze and drank it. Her canasta group's comin' over tonight and they don't have any . . . hee-hee . . . is's really funny."

"Ha!" said Freddy.

The cab slowed down and turned off the East Side Highway at 97th Street so J.D. could get out and go home. When we reached 19th Street fifteen minutes later, Slick was out cold. So while Freddy paid with Miss Otterbridge's money, we had to drag Slick out of the cab and then haul him over to his apartment house.

Jacqueline continued on in the cab. She lived in some hot place in Greenwich Village with a whole lot of roommates, boys and girls. A lot of actors share like that. Sounds good to me. . . .

When we finally got Slick up to his fourth-floor apartment and the door opened at our ring, his "mother" didn't think it was a bit funny to have him delivered that way.

Twenty-three

The day of the Dramafest, the Wartzburg bubbled over with talk. The old folks' eyes sparkled. J.D. noticed they walked "young."

"They're acting like they're all going to get presents tomorrow. It's Christmas Eve!" George said.

Miss Otterbridge had ordered a catered dinner. We ate an Italian feast shipped from the Milano restaurant, and sat with the residents, and didn't have to do any cleanup. Immediately afterward Sir Cecil sent me up to his own bathroom for my shower and shave.

"I've laid out fresh towels, Yardley soap, lilac Pinaud's after-shave, and some brilliantine for your unruly hair. It will give it luster and control. Use whatever you like in the medicine cabinet! Take your time. Relax . . ." He swept his hands up his chest expansively. "Prepare, my boy, for the great moments to come!"

His voice resonated in the dining room. I felt funny, but how could I refuse?

Up on the second floor it was quiet. People were getting ready in their rooms. Sir Cecil's bathroom was as big as our living room. The shower was hot and steamy; the towels, thick, thirsty, and monogrammed.

I skipped the brilliantine. It's greasier than Preparation H! But I slicked my wet hair down, plucked my eyebrows with Sir Cecil's tweezers from the medicine cabinet, and then put on the pants and buckled shoes to

my costume. Bare-chested, I clattered down the hall, hoping somebody'd hear me.

I was not disappointed. I heard a sexy whistle before I hit the stairs.

"Who's making that racket . . . Errol Flynn?" It was Pearl under a layer of cold cream poking her head out a door three down from Sir Cecil's. "Break a leg, kid!" she said.

"What?"

"In show biz, honey, it means *lotsa luck.* You deserve it."

What a madhouse it was backstage! Freddy and Alfonso were screaming at each other over the placement of the couch in *Streetcar.*

"Thees ees not where it was when I set the lights!" Alfonso said.

"Testing. Testing," George yelled over the intercom, and then drowned out the fight with a tape of the night noises of New Orleans he'd made for Flora and Gayle's play.

From the wings there was a glimpse of the auditorium with its gleaming chandeliers, gilded walls, and big, empty plush seats. At the sight of them I felt my throat constrict. I calmed down by reminding myself that it was only the folks from the Wartzburg and their families who would be in them. No critics or wolves!

Slick, already in his dance clothes, was at the door of the dressing room doing stretches. It was hot and crowded in there. J.D. was staring at himself in the full-length mirror, admiring his white tie and black tails, high hat and patent-leather shoes. He clicked his fingers and said, "Ain't I hot!"

I slid into the seat next to sweet Jacqueline. Miss

Otterbridge, in a sleazy flowered smock, was supervising her makeup.

"You want to run lines, Ace, while we get made up?" Jacqueline said, giving me a big smile.

"Don't think so! Ha-ha. That doesn't sound lucky." I slapped on the makeup base and then applied a stroke of black eyebrow pencil to my faint brow line. The bulbs around the mirror lit up every pore and zit like I was on an operating table. Where I'd been so tweezer happy, there were big, red, ugly splotches. Cover those with thick slabs of makeup, I thought.

"I don't want to mess up in front of *that* audience! We better run 'em," Jacqueline said.

I was beginning now to apply the putty to my nose. "What do you mean?"

J.D. said, "You know, man, who's going to be out there watchin' you, watchin' me, catchin' Slick. Woooo!"

I turned my head to look at him and bumped into Miss Otterbridge's hip. She was rouging Jacqueline and putting a black line in her cleavage.

"Who?" I said. "Miss Otterbridge, what are they talking about?"

"The board of directors is going to be here. Maybe that's what he means. They always come. Lovely people," she answered calmly.

"Who?"

"That putty's going to dry if you don't continue building up your nose." She patted it into a better shape.

"Just Helen Hayes, Ossie Davis, Robert Preston, Meryl Streep, Nathaniel McNamara, and Mickey Rooney," Slick said, bending down and touching his whole head to the floor.

"Mickey Rooney! He's my idol, after Nevada!" I said.

"Why didn't you tell me, Miss Otterbridge?" I was yelling and swiping at my greasepaint and unsticking my nose.

"I wasn't keeping it from you, Horace!" The wisps of her hair seemed to collect around her ears protectively. I wanted to knock her block off.

"I can't be Cyrano for *them!*"

She raised her hand to quiet me.

"No!" I said through chattering teeth. "They'll laugh. If not here, then later, in their homes."

Jacqueline saw what I'd done to my makeup and stopped outlining her wide eyes.

J.D. left the mirror. "Come on, you've lost your sense of perspective, Jack. They won't expect that much of you."

I stood up. "That's exactly what I mean!" I was fuming, practically foaming at the mouth like a trapped animal.

"Why didn't he know it?" Slick mumbled with his head practically sitting on the floor. "I heard it a long time ago. Everybody else knew the theater personages were going to be out there. That's why I wanted to do it!"

"Why didn't you tell me then?"

Everybody looked blank.

"Forget it!" I ripped off my makeup towel, kicked off the shoes, and unrolled the knee-length socks that had cost me eight bucks.

Miss Otterbridge, her face red, ran out of the room.

"Come on, Ace," Slick said, following me to the locker backstage where I'd stowed my jeans.

Jacqueline followed him and practically stood on my feet, blubbering and wiping her nose on the blue chiffon sleeve of her costume.

But I pulled on my shirt and sneakers. Forget the jeans. I'd change later. I was making my break.

"If you fail to go on that stage . . . my man," a booming voice rolled out behind me. "You are an *idiot!*"

Somebody had told Sir Cecil!

"Sir Cecil!" I squeaked, going up on my tiptoes and banging into the metal edge of my locker. "Ow!"

I shook my head no. I was not going on that stage for anybody!

"You think, do you, that you're different from anyone else who has taken the risk of going onstage?"

"I am scared!" I said, blasting him with honesty.

"Who cares!" he bellowed.

Why had I accepted this stupid role!

"Every artist tastes true terror," he said. "It's nothing. If you give in, you'll never mount the horse again."

He paused. An audience had gathered. Freddy and George were staring at me from the side.

I took a deep breath. He wasn't going to talk me into it.

"Your life will be a failure. You might as well commit suicide," he said, reaching out and pulling one of the cables supporting a flying backdrop to him. Then he took my clammy hand and put the rope into it. "Here is a rope. If you're not any good, afterward you can hang yourself."

The air rushed out of my lungs.

"Now the show must go on. The choice you made weeks ago is irrevocable. Get back in that dressing room now, or I'll kill you myself," he said softly.

Slick and Miss Otterbridge in tears were waiting there for me. When I came in, they left me alone and I fixed my makeup, restuck the nose, and put on my

costume. But I didn't feel any better. I was going to my doom.

Over the intercom I heard the Dramafest begin with PeeWee on piano. I knew J.D. was dancing. The applause they got sounded like it was a *big* audience.

"Oh . . . sh . . ."

Then I heard the scene with Flora and Gayle and it didn't even make me laugh. After the jugglers and the vaudeville sketch I walked the last mile to the stage, where the Bakery of the Poets was already in place. Freddy, with sweat running down his dark face, was piling cupcakes on the counter. Jacqueline had taken her place onstage. So had the other actors in it.

George put on the taped music that cued Sir Cecil's introduction of the play. I could hear the rustle of playbills and an occasional cough from the breathing audience as I heard him call Ace Hobart a "coming actor."

"I may be going out on a limb saying this, but Hobart has an ease on stage that is amazing."

Out on a limb? He just walked the plank!

The curtain rose on *Cyrano de Bergerac*. From the wings I glimpsed the audience and went numb.

The lines being spoken onstage seemed to float in outer space. I couldn't feel my hands. George came and stood on one side of me; Freddy, on the other.

The baker said onstage, "Make up your mind at last, Jack-o-Dreams!"

My cue.

I was aware of my breath rushing in and out of my body. My knees buckled and Freddy raised a glass of water and dashed it over my head. "Cut it—" I started to yell.

"Shhhh!" he said.

George shoved his fist in my back and said, "Go for it, pal!"

I stumbled forward, then caught the glare of the klieg lights as I strode on the stage in Cyrano's shoes with the weights. My head was sopping.

There was a terrific hush.

An absolute silence, as if the audience had suffocated.

The old actor playing the baker straightened in anticipation of my line. They were waiting. My eyes went from person to person and rested on Jacqueline, who smiled at me and raised her clasped hands to her terrific bosom. My voice came unstuck.

"What is the time!" I said in my deepest, richest voice.

From that moment on, I just became Cyrano.

The next thing I was conscious of was that the lights had faded and I was saying, "I stand not high, it may be, but alone!" My last line.

The stage went dark.

The curtain went down.

There was a burst of applause. "You did it! Listen to them," Jacqueline/Roxane at my side murmured. "Oh, Ace!" My heart thundered.

"It's over?" I said. She nodded. "Whoopee!" I threw up my arms. As the curtain opened again, I was jumping in the air.

The audience had caught me and laughed. But I didn't care. Jacqueline blew them a kiss and bowed, tugging my hand so that I dropped my head too.

"They loved it!" she whispered as we took bow after bow.

Back in the dressing room again—it hardly seemed I'd been gone—the time of being onstage had just dis-

appeared. Sir Cecil, waiting there, rose from his wheelchair and planted his hands on my head. "With mine
own hands, I give away my crown," he said, his voice
stirring with emotion.

"Hey, is that Shakespeare?" I said.

"You were good, my boy. They liked you. I'm sure
during the intermission they'll be talking of nothing
else."

They liked me, he said.

I was an actor?

Everybody came to me and told me so. The Falcons
were really excited. "You was highly prosmosigus!" Pee-
Wee said. "You made that old cat come alive. Pow!"

"A very sexy performance!" Pearl said.

Miss Otterbridge was still crying. "It was wonderful!"

Then *zap!* it was over.

The show went on. Freddy's bakery was struck from
the stage. Leslie, playing the mad Cassandra, was going
berserk, screaming and tearing out strands of her long
black wig.

I couldn't concentrate on that, though, because suddenly my performance came rushing back to me and I
lived it all over again. It was every bit as great as being
in the movie had been. I *liked* having a breathing, live
audience! It was like being on a wild roller coaster to
play a part in front of people.

I was a happy guy.

Slick's bit was the finale. I'd changed into my jeans
and T-shirt, removed the makeup, and gone into the
auditorium to catch him. As I came in, the audience
gasped.

What was happening?

Slick, in a glossy black body leotard, was about three

feet off the ground, casting a giant shadow on the ten-foot golden-orange sun that Freddy had built him as a backdrop.

"Seven . . . eight . . ." a woman in an aisle seat was whispering, counting the times Slick crossed and uncrossed his feet while up in the air.

How could he stay up that long? Was it a trick? Was he hung on a hook . . . or what?

The audience gasped again. Slick was down, gliding. Leaping.

Legs stretched in a horizontal split, parallel to the stage floor.

Wires? Freddy had rigged up a halter like they used in *Peter Pan?*

No, wait. If Slick was flying on wires, how could he turn like that, up on the toes of one foot, whip the other leg sharply sideways at the end of the revolution? . . .

And then he was break-dancing.

He made it look like the floor was moving, not himself!

Spinning! On his chest. On his hand.

The audience broke into applause, like an eruption of Mount Etna.

By the time the dance had ended, they were standing and cheering.

When he finished, he did a bow that swept the floor. He was a star! My old dumb buddy Slick, a born super-star!

At the reception in the dining room afterward, Miss Otterbridge introduced the chairman of the board, Mr. Nathaniel McNamara. The famous people, except for Ossie Davis, left before it even started. Like the big stars, all of us Falcons were dying to get out of there too.

It was boring. The guy gave a speech and went on and on. J.D. was nudging me and making cracks when suddenly the guy said something important.

"In the forty-seven-year history of the Dramafest, the Guild has presented this award to nine remarkably gifted actors and actresses, who each gave, as our recipient did tonight, a performance so luminous and confident that even as a singular creation it ennobled our art form. . . ."

J.D. burst out laughing.

But I didn't. What award, I wondered, nobody told me anything about an award.

"Ace Hobart dared to become one with the homeliness of the character he created. He dared to bring a living force on our stage . . . to make his character real. . . ."

Suddenly everybody at the Wartzburg was looking at me! Guests and all! Raven had a big smile on her face.

Mr. McNamara moved away from the microphone and came toward me.

"Hey, Ace! Way to go!" George said as McNamara in his navy blazer and striped tie presented me an envelope with a gold seal.

"Hi, Ace!" said the smooth McNamara. "It is my honor to present you with the Guild's Young Actors Scholarship Award."

"Thank you, sir!" I said, rising.

All the Falcons clapped and cheered. So did the Wartzburg residents.

"Go on, open it up."

I hope it's money, I thought, remembering I still owed on the darn Visa. "Oh! *Acting lessons every Saturday at The Neighborhood Playhouse!*" I said, sure it was

something good, but mortified because I'd never heard of the place.

"The best training in the city, Ace," Mr. McNamara said. "You'll flourish there."

I went over to Miss Otterbridge and immediately apologized for making her cry before I went onstage.

Funny thing is . . . her eyes got all teary all over again.

Belva Bithell and PeeWee gave me a hug. Gayle and Flora slipped me a twenty. "Buy the boys something to eat," they said.

There was one more award given. To Slick, for *dancing lessons.* He called up his mom before we even left the Wartzburg, he was so excited.

Afterward we didn't go for food. Funny, we were planning to eat in La Bombola China Grande, Piranhas or not!

But when we got there, the place had burned down and was boarded up. A cop on the beat said it had happened last night.

During dress rehearsal.

"Hey! That's awful," Slick said. "I liked those *colorados.*"

"Wonder if somebody found out about the fryman?" George said. "If it weren't so late, I'd call Pearl."

As we went to the subway, Raven said, "Guess what?"

"What?"

"How about you and me sneaking off? Ya know, somewhere private? We could go up to the roof of my building and see the stars. We can see if one says 'Ace' . . ."

"Hah!"

Funny, appealing as the idea was, I didn't want to go. I just wanted to stop off at the playground for PS 7 and play some two-on-two under the hoops. When I mentioned it to the other Falcons, they cheered.

Raven was understanding. "I should have realized you guys were all wound up. Listen, I'm really tired anyway and I want to get up early and take the twins to the zoo. So I'll see you, okay?" she said.

We dropped her off at her apartment before going to the school yard. "You're sure it's okay, Raven?" I said. I didn't want to completely lose out on the chance to be alone with her. "How about a movie next week and . . . uh . . . dinner. Okay?"

She nodded her head and went upstairs. Me and the guys headed for the hoops.

Twenty-four

Having a week of work left after the Dramafest was sort of an anticlimax—like eating cauliflower after finishing a hot fudge sundae. Nevertheless, I'd accomplished what Mom and the Visa people had set out for me to do over the summer. I'd paid off my bills.

Well, almost. All I had left was the balance due on my Gravity Guide System, which was still in a box hidden in the recesses of my closet. It was too late to send it back. The money for that would come out of my last paycheck, leaving me with better than a hundred bucks to blow. And how was I going to blow it? By taking Raven out to dinner in the most beautiful restaurant in New York.

"You're kidding, Ace! Tavern-on-the-Green . . . in Central Park?" she squealed when I asked her. "But isn't it terribly expensive?"

Expensive? Sure. So what. Nothing was too good for my girl. Hadn't she been my inspiration? My guiding star? The one with the modus operandi to get me to learn my Cyrano lines? Because of her, I had free tuition at The Neighborhood Playhouse.

I had it all planned. I'd make reservations for eight o'clock, Friday night. We'd go to the Tavern by taxi, have vichyssoise, shrimp cocktails, prime rib, and parfaits in tall glasses in the Crystal Room, and maybe, if a ten-spot could convince a waiter, look old enough to drink champagne. Afterward, we'd go for a horse-

drawn buggy ride through Central Park. Then after that? My pulse went haywire.

Meanwhile, up at the Wartzburg, I was in charge of some new trainees—five actors Miss Otterbridge had hired fresh out of the chorus line of *In a Pig's Eye*, the off-Broadway flop that closed during the intermission of its opening performance.

The trainees were to take over as waiters and gardeners once us Falcons returned to school after Labor Day. Freddy and Slick were responsible for getting them acquainted with things like Ortho weed killer, and it was my business to see that they knew where to set the bread plates and how to fold tea towels.

What a surly group! So sullen and testy—as if they thought going to work in an old folks home was demeaning. George and I got so fed up hearing them bellyache about doing small stuff like cutting up meat, we were tempted to tell Miss Otterbridge she ought to ship the whole lot of them back to Jerry Cone's office. And I think we would have, too, if Slick hadn't intervened.

"Look, Ace . . . George! Give 'em a break," he told us. "These guys are real depressed. Know what I mean? Wasn't their fault Jerry Ice Cream steered them into doing a bum show. They'll get to like it here, same as we did."

Slick's tolerance had a lot to do with the Little Mary Sunshine mental state he'd been in since the Dramafest. Unbeknownst to him, Miss Otterbridge had invited some ballet bigwigs to come watch him dance, and now he was booked for auditions till the middle of September. His only real worry was his name. Slick, he'd concluded, didn't sound "smooth" enough to use professionally unless he was accepted by an avant-

garde dance company like Twyla Tharp's. "If I'm not,"
he said, "I'm gonna call myself Pierre-Antoine."

On Friday, our last day at the Wartzburg, Miss Otterbridge let J.D., George, and me come to work with
Freddy and Slick in the morning so we could leave
early with them in the afternoon. For the first time,
Lance, Chad, and Derrick, the three new waiters re-
placing us, would be on their own to serve dinner.

Our sulky, sullen trainees didn't appreciate any of
the hard-earned expertise we'd passed on, however.
They didn't thank us, didn't wish us well or bother to
shake hands. Even Slick was ticked off, so at George's
suggestion we invented some "inside tips" we thought
would make their new jobs more interesting.

Freddy and Slick gave the two gardeners a list of food
scraps they claimed were absolute essentials for a de-
cent garden compost heap. Underlined was *anything
partially chewed.* "Just scrape it off the plates and save
it," said Freddy.

"Then when it turns black, pack it under the rose-
bushes or they'll die," Slick added.

"And if the five of you don't want to carry home
institutional odors," J.D. advised, "you gotta use
oatmeal. Just ask Mister Raymond to save you what's
left from breakfast. Then before you go home, rub it in
a thick paste all over your arms, necks, and faces. Let it
dry, then rinse off. I learned about it from an Avon
representative."

"Nothing else works," said Freddy.

George smiled. "Except lye."

"And whatever you do, don't lose Jerry Cone as your
agent," it was my turn to tell them. "He's the choice of

stars. The very best in the business. Voted the number-
one favorite by every single Broadway producer."

George was waiting. His inside tip was the last we'd
rehearsed.

"Just one more thing," he said, pulling a map he'd
drawn out of his pocket. "If you ever want a good meal
in the Bronx, this'll show you how to get to a top-notch
place called, La Bombola China Grande."

Then, right out of the blue, Slick made up a tip of his
own:

"Don't forget to look up our best buddies here," he
said. "They're a singing group called the Piranhas. If
you tell 'em you're friends of ours, they'll show you a
real good time."

Miss Otterbridge got pretty choked up saying good-
bye to us when we went into her office to pick up our
paychecks.

"You young men are among the best employees
we've ever had," she said, dabbing under her glasses
with a tissue. "Reliable. Courteous. Trustworthy. And I
. . . I am going to miss you very much."

In addition to our paychecks, she presented each of
us with a personal gift—embossed stationery from
Cartier. Mine was pale blue with my initials, HNH, in
navy at the top. She'd found out my middle name.
Nelson. One of my deepest secrets.

"Hey, this is real classy stuff," Freddy said. "You're a
real lady, Miss Otterbridge."

". . . If you're ever in a pinch for waiters on weekends, give us a call," George cut in. "We'll be available."

"I'll do that," she said. "I most certainly will."

She walked us to the front door and when we opened
it, we were bowled over by what we saw. A lineup that

went clear across the porch, down the steps, and half-way down the walk. Every employee and resident of the Wartzburg, except for our replacements and Pearl, who'd been called to California to tape Merv Griffin's show, was in it.

A little group standing with the housekeepers, closest to the door, seemed confused and couldn't quite place who we were, but each of the others had something to say as we passed.

Whar Ma Bleedin' From tipped his hat to me. "Shore gits hot in these here Hawaiian huts," he said, looking up from his rocker.

"Sure does," I said.

J.D. got a kiss on the cheek from Leslie, plus a note with her address and home phone number. He was so light-headed, he nearly walked right by PeeWee. "Hey! Jes' a minute, Jack! Hold it!" PeeWee hollered. "I gots something to give you." He pulled off his black derby and slapped it on J.D.'s head. "There, Jack! That's for when you shuffles off to Buffalo."

"Buffalo? You kidding, man? From now on, this hat goes *anywhere* I go," J.D. hooted.

Alfonso grinned as he shook our hands. *"Vayan con Dios, amigos.* Chew all come back and see us berry, berry soon. Hokay, dokay?"

"Sure shootin'," we chimed.

Mister Raymond gave each of us a bag of oven-fresh pecan sandies to eat on our way home, and Belva Bithell, who only had eyes for Slick, curtsied when he approached her. "Farewell, Mr. President," she said in her tremulous ninety-three-year-old voice. "It was with profound regret that we learned you would not be running a second term."

"Well, it's like this, Miss Bithell . . . I couldn't run,

ya see. I got lotsa pressing matters elsewheres," Slick
said.

She nodded solemnly. "So I hear, Mr. President."

Jacqueline, who was with her, wished me luck at The
Neighborhood Playhouse, and Sir Cecil, sitting in his
wheelchair, made a grand gesture of getting out of it to
present me with a 1947 British playbill. "That was the
first season I played King Lear in London," he said,
motioning to the picture of himself with a scraggly
white beard on the cover.

To H. Hobart, my heir apparent, he'd written at the
bottom. *Always remember: The play's the thing.*

C. Bancroft

"Keep the playbill," he said, "as a reminder that you
are expected to come back to next year's Dramafest so I
may direct you in the title role."

"How very presumptuous of you!" Flora screeched at
him.

"Yes, indeed. Very presumptuous!" echoed Gayle.
"Mr. Hobart will come back to play Stanley. For *us!*"

"Not on your lives," thundered Sir Cecil.

"Oh, we shall see, you bloody, arrogant old . . ."

They were still squabbling when the five of us Falcons went past the guardhouse and out the front gate.
The watchman waved. "You weirdos take care of your-
selves, ya hear?" he called after us.

"We will," we yelled.

What a send-off. I was feeling pretty overwhelmed at
the sight of all those old people coming out to say good-
bye to us and I tried walking a step ahead of the others.
I thought they'd tease me if they saw my eyes well up.

"Damn pollen count," said Freddy. "It's giving me an
allergy."

"Yeah, me too," sniffed George.

I rode the subway with them down to 23rd Street in Manhattan but said I'd have to beg off when they invited me to join them for a pizza at Mario's. Tonight was my big night with Raven. I had important things to attend to: First, I had to cash my paycheck at Gristede's. Then I was taking a bus down to the Jock Shop, on 8th Street, to pay off my Gravity Guide System. What a relief! Now I could use the thing.

"Here you go, Ace . . . two hundred thirty-four dollars and sixty-two cents," Mom's boss, Mr. Papadopoulos, said when he closed his cash register and handed me my money.

I folded all those crisp greenbacks into a nice thick wad, stuck them in my pocket, and thanked him.

"You be careful now, walking around with all that cash," he warned. "Muggers have a way of smelling it, you know."

Well, he needn't have worried. When I got on the bus, it was jam-packed and the only seat available was way in the back, next to a nun. Not a modern-day nun, either. She came from an old-fashioned, conservative order. I could tell by her full-length habit.

I almost laughed. Wouldn't Mom be pleased?

I took the empty seat, looked at my watch, and sighed. In two hours I'd be riding in a taxi to pick up the goddess of J. F. Kennedy High. She'd be wearing her new peach silk dress. She'd bought it just for the occasion; for our night at Tavern-on-the-Green. Ah! What a vision of loveliness, I knew already. Maybe I'd buy her flowers. Why not? I was loaded.

I sighed again. I could hardly wait. Shrimp. Prime ribs. A romantic ride through Central . . . *gee, that*

nun has big feet! Real man-size clodhoppers . . . Park
in a horse-drawn buggy. I'd always wanted to do that.
Ever since I'd moved to New York last year, I'd wanted
. . . *and such fat, dirty, stubby fingers. Ewww. With
black hairs growing around the knuckles!*

My eyes spun up to the face. Five o'clock shadow? On
a nun?

"Okay, buster. Don't let out a peep," she—*he*, rather
—whispered, poking something hard in my ribs. "I got
a gun on ya."

A mugger! I'd sat next to a #¶**!§&* mugger! Why?
How? Things like this didn't happen to Ace Hobart.
Only to *other* people!

"Get off ahead of me, next stop. Then walk to the
corner and hand me everything ya got. Watch. Wallet.
Any funny business and pigeons'll be eating yer brains
fer dinner. Got that?"

I swallowed. "Yes, Sister."

"Okay, we're stopping. Get up."

He stayed a hairsbreadth behind me, ready to blast
out my kidney as I slowly minced my way to the door.
Help! Somebody help me! Couldn't the other passengers tell what was happening? *Help! Please help!* Don't
let him take all my hard-earned money. Or my watch.
My beautiful digital waterproof, shockproof three-hun-
dred-dollar watch!

"Okay, buster. Down the steps!"

I looked back, pleadingly, at the busload of people.
Nobody else was getting off with us. Not *one* other
person!

"Okay. Now head for the corner."

Epilogue

Raven and I ate hamburgers at McDonald's that night. She refused to see me or speak to me ever again.

Wait! Hold it

THAT'S NOT WHAT ACTUALLY HAPPENED . . .

It's only what I *thought* would happen when the thug pushed me off the bus and nobody was down on the street corner.

Lost! . . . the romantic night of my dreams! Gone forever, I thought as I handed the creep my watch. I nearly bawled. Then something snapped in my head. This wasn't going to happen to me! *Oh, no!* Not to somebody who's spent half his life practically memorizing eighteen Nevada Culhane books.

"Hand over your wallet," said Bigfoot.

I stared him straight in the eye as I dipped into my pocket. I was thinking. That scene from *Say Your Prayers* . . . when Nevada was surrounded by a tribe of savage headhunters. What'd he done? What? *Acted crazy!*

"I said, hand it over, buster!"

Well, here goes. First the sick laugh. *"Eeeeeeee-ahhhh, gluck, gluck . . . yeh-heh-heh-heh, ah-ha-ha-*

ha, tee-hee-hee-hee-heeeeeee!" (Hey! Even better than
Flame and Ember.) *"Eeeeeeeee-hee-heeee ha-ha gluck!"*

Stop! Mouth open; out with the tongue. Drool and do
googly eyes. Roll 'em. Round and around and around.
Clockwise. Counterclockwise. Now cross 'em. Uncross
'em. Stop! Now the head goes bobbing. Bob, bob, bob-
bity, bob, bob . . . and the arms start flapping. Flap,
flap, flappity, flap, flap!

And now the jungle-vulture mating call: *Yukka,
yukka, blaaawk, blaaawk! Chirri-cheee chee chee chee*
. . . *Yukka, chee, chirri, blaaawk, blaaawk!* I bobbed
and flapped, screeched and squawked, then threw myself on the sidewalk, rolling, kicking, flailing my arms,
and still drooling.

Was Bigfoot buying it? I peeked up to see. Jeez, he
was! He'd backed off like I was in the last stages of
rabies. Okay! Ready for step number two: *Get up and
chase him!*

I sprang off the ground, into the air, adding some
fancy swashbuckling Cyrano footwork to my mad-dog
Nevada. "Charge!" I roared. Nothing was in my hand,
but I held it high above my head and lunged after him,
grinning and cackling like I couldn't wait to rip him
apart.

"Help! Somebody help me!!" he screamed.

I never saw anybody in a long black skirt run faster. I
kept after him all the way over to Avenue B, stopping
when I heard him drop something. My watch? Nope. A
six-inch piece of pipe. The old faker! He'd never had a
gun.

I did find my watch, though. It was lying next to the
stoop of a tenement house a few feet away. When I bent
down to pick it up, I heard somebody shouting,
"Wicked heathen!" I looked up and saw a wizened

white-haired woman leaning out her window, shaking her fist at me. "You'll burn forever for what you've done!"

"That wasn't a real nun," I called.

She gave me the sign of the cross and slammed her window shut.

I didn't go down to Zero's to pay the balance on my Gravity Guide System. I forgot. With all that adrenaline surging through my body, I cooled off by jogging twenty blocks to get home. My watch crystal was broken, but so what? My romantic evening with Raven was spared. I had all my money.

Man, was a hot shower going to feel good! Nearly every inch of me was covered with gunk I'd picked up from rolling on the sidewalk. Even the side of my head felt gooey.

I raced up the stairs to The Pits, opened the door, and was greeted by Nora.

"Eeewww! What happened to you?" she said.

"I darn near got mugged."

"Liar! Think I can't see? A bird pooped in your hair."

Loud hee-hawing came from the living room when she said that. "Who's here? The Falcons?" I asked.

"Guess again."

To make a long story short, six Piranhas were waiting for me. Stab, Cannibal, Turtle, and three other Neanderthals, making themselves at home, eating the chips and dip Nora had served them. I couldn't believe how she'd kept them entertained. I could've killed her.

"Gimme that!" I said, snatching one of my baby pictures out of Cannibal's hands.

Stab held his fingers in the peace sign. "Look, Ace. No

offense, okay? We see you're still sore 'cause of the scam
we pulled."

"Scam? Ha-ha. You think *I* didn't know who the police commissioner was?"

"This time it ain't no trick," said Turtle. "We know
stuff that'll make us all a bundle." He pulled some tis-
sues out of his pocket. "For your hair," he said, trying
not to look at it. "How does splittin' twenty-five G's
sound?"

I blotted my head. "I'm not interested."

"I am. Tell *me!*" said Nora.

"You get out of here and go in your room," I yelled.
"Or else I'll drag you in there!"

"Hey!" boomed two-ton Cannibal. "Quit pickin' on
her. She's a cute little kid!"

Nora made a dollface smile for him. "I wish *you* were
my big brother." Then to me she said, "Okay, nincom-
birdpoophead. I'll go!"

But, of course, she didn't. She just walked out of the
room, then stayed in the hall, pretending she'd gone.

"So?" I said, facing the Piranhas again. "What's your
line this time? Hard-core proof? That you know for a
fact who's heading the arson ring?"

They all nodded, ignoring my stinging sarcasm. Then
this hollow-cheeked guy, Stockingcap spoke up. "Ya
see, Ace, we can't squeal on her on account of one of us
has . . ."

I snickered. "Oh, it's a *her* this time?"

"Right. A broad," he said. "And one of us has a relative who's mixed up with her. He fixed it so two of her
buildings burned."

"Us Piranhas swore to a loyalty oath," Stab added.
"Squealing on family's a violation. Know what I mean?"

"Oh, yeah. Sure, sure. You'd be traitors if *you* went to

the police. But it's okay to tell me so *I* can go. What's the difference?"

"A big one!" he said, looking indignant.

I shook my head. "Man, you dudes are incredible."

But not half as incredible as the rest of their story. What baloney. Their so-called relative was a handyman, they said. Someone who'd worked in the Bronx for years and knew the insides of dozens and dozens of buildings. He'd drawn blueprints of the electrical systems in two of the burned-out buildings. The two, naturally, that later caught fire because of their "faulty" wiring.

"After each fire he collected five thousand bucks," Turtle said. *"In cash* from Iris Welch. See the connection?"

I howled. "You mean you guys are saying *Iris Welch,* the founder of the Bronx Model Youth League, is the mastermind? The lady who passes out Kool-Aid and graham crackers?" I doubled over laughing. "That's gotta be the best joke I've heard in years."

"It ain't funny!" Stab snapped. "She's either owner or part owner of fifteen slum buildings. We checked her out. And Cannibal here lives in one. Maybe it'll go up in smoke next."

I glanced at my watch. "Well, it's been real good fun talking to y'all. But now I'm gonna say *adiós.* In two hours I've got me a date with Miss Universe."

I started to walk out, leaving them sitting by themselves. Then I looked back. "Just one more question. How come none of the punk girls ever squealed on Iris Welch? Did ya figure that out?"

"Yeah, we did," said the guy who up till then had kept his mouth shut. "The punks never knew who they was working for. They'd get agnimos . . ."

"Anonymous," said Stab.

"Right. Agniminos phone calls telling them where to strike. When they'd done it, they'd get money in the mail."

I winked and gave him the A-OK sign. "Gotta hand it to ya. You're creative storytellers."

Then I went in the bathroom and took a long, hot shower. (And shampooed my hair, of course.)

The REAL Epilogue

My romantic evening with Raven was better than any in my wildest dreams. We had a table for two on the garden patio at Tavern-on-the-Green. She ordered lobster, I ordered filet mignon. It was juicy and rare in the middle, just how I like it. But I hardly ate a bite. I was too busy looking at Raven. Her peach silk dress was perfect—gave a soft glow to her face under the patio lanterns. But the two white gardenias knocked me out most. She'd tucked them in her hair, just above the spot where it tumbles in waves down to her shoulder.

For dessert we had chocolate mousse. (I didn't eat much of that, either.) Then afterward we took a moonlight buggy ride through Central Park. And after that? Well, all I can say is this . . . *she's some kisser!* Whew.

P.S. Nora, the copycat, bought herself a water bed exactly like mine. Paid for it out of her share of the reward money she collected for turning in Iris Welch. The Piranhas were for real. Stab's stepfather was the relative.

About the Authors

BARBARA BEASLEY MURPHY is the author of *Thor Heyerdahl and the Reed Boat Ra* (with Norman Baker), *No Place to Run, One Another,* and *Love Lives On.* She lives in New Rochelle, New York.

JUDIE WOLKOFF is the author of *Wally, Where the Elf King Sings,* and *Happily Ever After . . . Almost.* She lives in Hastings-on-Hudson, New York.